A Veiled
Antiquity

A Veiled Antiquity

A NOVEL BY

RETT MACPHERSON

ST. MARTIN'S PRESS

NEW YORK

Library of Congress Cataloging-in-Publication Data

MacPherson, Rett.
    A veiled antiquity : a novel / by Rett MacPherson. — 1st ed.
      p.   cm.
    ISBN 0-312-18677-0
    I. Title.
PS3563.A3257V45   1988   98-6929
813'.54—dc21   CIP

First Edition: June 1998

10 9 8 7 6 5 4 3 2 1

To my mother,

Lena Blanche Justice

Thank you for watching old Agatha Christie
movies with me and trying to figure out
"whodunnit" first. You planted the seed.

Acknowledgments

I wish to acknowledge and thank the people who helped me get through the process of this book.

Thank you to my incredible friends who got me through this past year-and-a-half of my life! It hasn't been easy. Thank you to Regina Hensley, lifelong friend, for holding my hand, wiping my tears, warding off evildoers, and giving the endless advice over and over. You never get tired of reassuring me. Thank you to Laurell K. Hamilton, for listening and agreeing with me when I needed you to, and offering such generous and selfless acts of friendship all the time; to Nikki Bess, for the midnight pep talks on the front porch; and to Matt Hawthorne and Beth McNeilly, who both have a certain calming effect on me, something I always desperately need.

Thank you to Joe Lange, who waltzed into my life and unveiled a world of peace and beauty. It was there all along, I just needed the right person to show it to me.

Thank you to my critique group, the Alternate Historians: Tom Drennan, N. L. Drew, Laurell K. Hamilton, Deborah Millitello, Marella Sands, and Mark Sumner; and the newcomers to our group, Gus Elliott and Sharon Shinn, who, so far, haven't seemed to mind our discussions about serial killers and rare flesh-eating viruses. Welcome to the madness.

Thank you to Ms. Sylvia Gant, high school history teacher extraordinare who introduced many historical mysteries to me.

And special thanks to a fellow St. Louisan—my wonderful editor, Kelley Ragland, who is both beautiful and smart. Thank you for making this almost painless.

And last but not least, my agent, Ricia Mainhardt.

A Veiled
Antiquity

One

I marched across the street still in my vintage clothing from the tour I had just finished. I wore a pink paisley-print gown with wide lapels, a high neck, puffed sleeves, and straight skirt. On my head was a large flowered hat that matched the dress. In one hand I carried a lace-trimmed parasol. In the other hand was a copy of the town newspaper.

I was a woman on a mission.

My mission was to find and strangle Eleanore Murdoch, the town gossip and inkslinger. She and her husband Oscar owned the Murdoch Inn, which sported a glorious view of the Mississippi River. Eleanore also had a teeny-weeny column in the *New Kassel Gazette* that caused more trouble than it did good. She fancied herself a writer of the highest degree. Nobody in town agreed with her, except maybe Oscar.

I walked determinedly down River Point Road, watching Old Man River roll along with the enthusiasm of a languid mule and noting in the air the faint evidence of the changing of the seasons.

It was September in New Kassel, Missouri. September in Missouri is usually one of two things: extremely hot or extremely cold. Missouri is never down the middle of anything except the continent. Today, however, was extremely nice.

The shops and houses bordered the street on my right, the river ran on my left, and the Murdoch Inn sat directly ahead at the end of the street. It was not the oldest building in New Kassel, but it was definitely the most delightful. Alexander Queen had it built in the 1880s. A porch with particularly delicate lattice and spiral works wrapped around the large, two-story Victorian building. The building was white with two turrets and an attic that had been renovated for use as guest rooms in addition to the rooms on the second floor.

I marched up the front steps of the inn with a copy of the last issue of the *New Kassel Gazette* under my left arm. I opened the door, found several guests lounging in the cozy, peach-colored living room, and couldn't help but think how ridiculous I must look. A few guests waved, recognizing me.

I am the tour guide for the historic buildings in New Kassel. I deck out in vintage clothing, even the shoes. I'm also a member of the Historical Society, and as a result, I'm often recognized by the tourists. I waved back at the guests seated on the ecru-colored sofa, sipping tea from a silver tea set that sat on a mahogany table.

Shoes clopping on the wooden floor, I walked on until I found the hallway that led to the small office where the customers checked in. Gilt-colored mirrors hung on cream-colored walls, with the doorways and woodwork trimmed in stark white. I entered the office, rang the tinny-sounding bell on the desk, and tapped my foot while I waited.

Out came Eleanor Murdoch from another door in the room. Now, I will give her some credit. Her column, until the last few months, had never been vicious. Inquiring to the point of invading privacy perhaps, but never vicious. She was overstepping ethical boundaries now. At least, my ethical boundaries.

She's about forty-five, top-heavy, with a pretty face but terrible taste in jewelry. Big, bulky costume jewelry was all she ever wore, and it seemed as though she wore every piece she had all at one time.

She knew exactly why I was there, but still she smiled and said, "Hello, Torie. What can I do for you?"

Almost everybody calls me Torie. Not even my husband Rudy calls me Victory. My two daughters of course call me Mom, except when my oldest tried for a time to get by with calling me Victory. The only people who call me that are my mother and Sylvia Pershing. Both are women of consequence.

Eleanore stood with her hands clasped on the desk of the office, waiting for me to return her socially correct behavior, which I couldn't do even if I hadn't been completely furious with her. Most people who go by the laws of etiquette are actually as rude as the rest of us. They just disguise it.

I took a deep breath and swore I wouldn't call her any names. I wouldn't call her anything like hypocritical, vainglorious, snotty, gossiping battle-ax. No, nothing like that.

"Eleanore," I began as I spread the newspaper out on the counter for her. "Perhaps you'd like to explain the meaning of this."

Her brown eyes barely flicked down to the newspaper. "I was hoping you could explain it a little more to me," she said as she pulled a pencil and paper out of the top drawer. She was actually preparing to take notes. "I'm missing the finer points that are required to form the illiterate details of good writing."

"Literary."

"What?" she asked.

3

"You mean, literary details."

"Whatever. Get on with it," she said.

"There is nothing to tell."

She noted something on her paper. "It's all true. Your mother is having an affair with Sheriff Colin Brooke," she said, quite pleased with herself.

"She is not having an affair, Eleanore. She's divorced. He's divorced. They are two free people. Therefore it's not an affair. She is . . . his friend."

"Well, I can't very well print *friend* in my column. It's boring," she replied.

"But it's the truth."

"Torie, Torie, Torie," she said. "This is journalism. Nobody wants the truth. Or at least if they do, they want a stretched-out, barely recognizable facility of the truth."

"That's facsimile, Eleanor. Facsimile of the truth."

She was focused as she went on like a detective reciting the facts. "On the night of August thirtieth, your mother was seen in the presence of one Sheriff Colin Brooke, leaving the movie theater."

"She was?" I asked. Sheriff Brooke is about twelve years younger than my mother. I think that I'm open-minded enough to get past the fact that my mother is involved in a May/December relationship. But Sheriff Brooke actually arrested me one time. I suppose what really bothers me is that my mother doesn't seem to have the least bit of loyalty where this issue is concerned. Of course, I could be overreacting and being slightly childish, as my mother has so delicately brought to my attention on several occasions.

"Yes," Eleanore said. "They were seen leaving the theater, just after seeing the new Sean Connery flick."

Sean Connery? That could only mean one thing. Mother

had left the theater with a rapid pulse and labored breathing and not at all in her right state of mind. It would have been a perfect opportunity for the sheriff to take advantage of her.

"Eleanore, I don't care what facts you have to corroborate your column. I want a retraction. No beating around the bush. What my mother does is her own affair. It's not to be exploited like in the *Enquirer*. It makes it seem as though she is doing something wrong. If you want a job on *Hard Copy*, go get one. If you ever print anything about another member of my family that is less than complimentary, or less than the truth, I'll . . ."

"You'll what?"

I wasn't sure what I could do. "I'll start my own column," I said.

"But, Torie. That's not fair. If I can't write about your family that will severely limit my subject matter. You're related to half of the town."

"I am not," I defended myself.

"Yes, you are," she whined and stomped her foot gently.

"Just drop it. I mean it. I want a retraction."

Just then the doors of the Murdoch Inn burst open. A very distressed Tobias Thorley swept past the shocked patrons and into the office.

"Torie," he said. "You've got to find the sheriff," he said to me.

"Calm down, Mr. Thorley. What's the problem?"

Tobias is our resident accordion player. Every German tourist town has to have an accordian player. And he is quite good. He's about seventy years old, spare as a scarecrow, with a large hook nose and kind blue eyes. He also has a great pair of legs that I've seen on many occasions when he wears his Bavarian knicker outfit.

"It's Marie Dijon," he said. "Ransford Dooley just found her at the foot of her basement steps. She's dead."

•

Nothing like a death to get people out of their houses.

I'd called 911 from the Murdoch Inn. The sheriff's office is located in Wisteria, which is about ten miles southwest of New Kassel. It serves the entire county, which is filled with tiny towns, Wisteria being the largest at a population of about four thousand.

I arrived at the home of Marie Dijon, on the corner of Hanover Road and Hermann Road. It was directly across from the firehouse, catty-corner to the New Kassel Cemetery, and next door to Pierre's Bakery on one side and a private residence on the other. It was a story-and-a-half brick home, of no real grandeur, but nice nonetheless.

The paramedics brought out Marie Dijon's body covered with a sheet. They put the gurney into the back of an ambulance and shut the door. At least half of the population of New Kassel was crammed onto the streets trying to get a glimpse of what was going on, though everybody kept their distance.

Deputy Edwin Duran looked around, saw a friendly face in the crowd, which just happened to be mine, and walked over.

"Hey, Torie," he said. "You workin'?"

"What?" I asked, confused. Then I remembered the clothes. "Oh, well, I just finished up and hadn't changed my clothes yet." I received no strange looks from the people in the crowd. They were used to seeing me like this.

"Who called this in?" he asked.

Why did he automatically think that I'd know who called this in? Of course I did, but that's not the point. I suppose I have sort of developed a reputation of knowing everything that transpires in New Kassel.

"I did."

"Did you find her?" he asked.

"No. Ransford Dooley found her. He's really shook up. He's over at the firehouse with Elmer."

Edwin is a few years older than I am. That would put him at about thirty-five. He has a thin, dark mustache, with hair of the same color, piercing blue eyes, and large ears. He looks spiffy in his deputy's uniform. I remember when he was the all-star quarterback for Meyersville High. New Kassel pounded them into the ground every time we played them.

"Is he ever going to retire?" Edwin said.

"Elmer? He's been the fire chief forever. He says he's going to retire but he never does."

"He's been saying it for about ten years now," Edwin said with a smile.

"I know. Poor guy."

Edwin glanced around at the crowd. "I swear," he said as he shook his head. "You could put dancing midgets on hot pink rubber balls, breathing fire and nailing spikes up their noses, and it wouldn't bring out the kind of crowd that one simple dead body brings."

"True." He was right. What more could I add to that? "So? What's it look like?" I asked.

"What? The body? Oh, she just fell down the steps. Older people do that."

"Marie Dijon was not that old," I challenged.

"How old was she? I don't know that much about her."

"She just moved here about two years ago. I'd say she's in her mid-fifties. That's not incredibly old, you know."

"People lose their balance all the time and fall. There was no

7

forced entry, no sign of a struggle. She just fell down the steps. She was still in her nightclothes."

"Where was she when Mr. Dooley found her?"

"All the way at the bottom. Her neck was all twisted around so that you could see her face even though she was on her stomach. Wasn't pretty, I'll tell you that."

"Hmph," was all I said. I thought for a moment. "Her nightclothes? Do you mean, pajamas, or pajamas with a housecoat and slippers?"

"She had on a housecoat, one slipper was on her foot and the other one was found about midway down the steps. Why?"

I didn't get a chance to answer him. Just then Sheriff Colin Brooke pulled up in his yellow Festiva. The Lone Ranger rides again. He got out, took one quick look at me, and hit himself in the forehead with his open palm.

The sheriff is fortyish, has sandy hair and blue eyes. He gives the impression of being a big strapping boy. In fact he is about six feet. He rarely seems to be in uniform. I usually see him in jeans and T-shirt. He has muscular arms, and looks ticked off all the time. Well, at least around me he looks ticked off all the time. I don't know what his problem is. After all, I did solve a case for him. One in which I lost a tooth and had to have a bridge put in.

"Torie, what the hell are you doing here?"

Edwin looked a little taken aback by the sheriff's demeanor and decided to stick up for me. "Well, she called in the nine-one-one."

Brooke stared at me for the longest time, and I knew what he was thinking before he even said it. Finally, when he could stand holding his tongue no longer, he said, "Please, tell me that you did not find this body."

"No," I said. "I didn't."

8

"Ransford Dooley found the body, Sheriff," Edwin said.

"Where were you?" I asked. "We wanted you to come riding up on your gallant steed and save the city."

"I was at your house," he answered me. "Having lunch with your mother."

I glanced around nervously and could see Eleanore Murdoch with her stupid notepad and her stupid pen standing on the edge of the pavement. Just what I needed. Surprisingly, almost every face that I found in the crowd was a native of New Kassel. I couldn't see one tourist.

"You don't have to announce it to the whole town," I said.

"Hey, everybody!" he yelled, as if he were going to shout it to the town.

I didn't find him amusing. I slugged him a good one just under his rib cage and he shut up, but not before having a really hearty laugh at my expense.

"Jerk," I mumbled.

All the while, Edwin watched us, unsure of what to do. I wanted to tell him that the sheriff and I were basically teasing each other. Basically.

"Edwin," he said. "Do not under any circumstances let Mrs. O'Shea know any of the details pertaining to the death of Ms. Dijon," he said.

Edwin swallowed and looked at his feet.

"Do I make myself clear?"

"Yes, of course."

Too late now. But what the sheriff doesn't know won't hurt him. I decided to slip out of the circus quietly and walk home. From Marie's house all I had to do to get home was walk a few blocks east on Hanover, hang a left on River Point Road, and a few houses later I would be home.

I was happy that I had decided to walk home because it gave

me time to think. So far in all of this mess, I hadn't thought about the one person who had lost her life on this day and that was Marie Dijon. I can't say that I knew Marie intimately, but I knew her as well as you could know an acquaintance in a couple of years' time. I had spoken to her on several occasions and I believe she was even at the opening of our museum this summer.

I did not know anything about her of a personal nature. She was not a native of New Kassel, and in a town where three-quarters of the population is native, the nonnatives stick out. I would go so far as to say that she was not from this region of the state at all, quite possibly not even Missouri.

I'd never seen a guest of any kind at her home and never heard her speak of a family member. That was the most tragic part of all, I thought. Nobody would mourn her passing.

Two

My husband, Rudy O'Shea, sat down on the edge of the bed and I studied him for a moment. He can be loud and obnoxious, but not nearly as much as I can be, so I try not to harp on it. He's naive and a genuine all-around good guy. He's only about five feet ten, which goes well with my five feet two, and he has chocolate brown eyes with a long face.

He's Irish, even though I know there is German in his family tree. I started tracing his lineage and his mother ordered me to stop. Any blood that's not Irish, they don't claim. Especially any blood that isn't Catholic Irish. Basically, my mother-in-law doesn't claim me because I'm neither of the two.

Rudy can tell anybody anything they want to know about holy days, holy weeks, how many candles to light for what, and any tidbit of information about saints and martyrs, especially if it's kind of gross. He can even name the popes in order.

But I'll be damned if he can tell you where the Battle of Jericho was fought.

He's not been to confession in several years and even longer since he went to church. I think the last time he went to confession was to confess that he hadn't been to church. Anyway, his mother of course blames this on me, along with our children's less-than-pure bloodline, of which I am wholeheartedly and completely innocent.

Rudy and I met in a hardware store where I was working. I was standing on a ladder in the hardware aisle and he was buying a drill. He swears that he was so taken with my shapely legs that he didn't realize he was walking straight into the ladder. He knocked it over and I crashed. Our first date was in the hospital when he wheeled me down to the cafeteria for chicken-fried steak, which I detest, but it was the thought that counted. He insisted on paying for it, because after all he was responsible for my broken leg. I think I fell in love with him at that moment.

This morning, he had accompanied me to the funeral of Marie Dijon.

"I can't thank you enough for going to Marie's funeral with me," I said to Rudy. He took off his tie and placed it neatly on his chest of drawers, next to the 5×7 photograph of our two daughters.

"Well, I wish I hadn't," he declared.

"Why?"

"That was the weirdest funeral I've ever been to. Nobody cried," he said.

"Well, none of us knew her that well. I'm sure we're all sad to see her go, but I didn't know her well enough to cry."

"Yeah, but no family members cried," he said.

"I didn't see any family members. I only saw about six or seven people that I didn't recognize. It was weird. And if you hadn't gone with me, Bernice Thorley would have insisted that I attend the funeral luncheon."

Rudy sat on the bed and pulled off his shoes. He reminded me of a child because he didn't untie them first. Instead he pulled and yanked and tugged until the shoe came flying off. I could have told him to untie his shoes first, but after ten years of marriage, if he wanted to keep his shoes tied when he took them off, so be it.

"What were you and Bernice Thorley discussing during the funeral, anyway?" he asked.

"I wasn't talking," I said. "I was listening. She went on and on about how unusual Marie's will was." I took my right high-heeled shoe off with the help of my left foot, and then did the reverse with the left shoe.

"How so?" Rudy said.

"Well, everything is to be auctioned. Only a citizen or business owner of New Kassel will be allowed to bid on it. No outsiders."

I was sitting at my dressing table. I took off my small silver earrings and noticed that Rudy watched me from the other side of the room. "What?" I said.

"You should wear that dress more often," he answered.

"It's too short," I said. "But I had nothing else in black."

"I know it's too short," he said. He smiled like a schoolboy. "That's why you should wear it more often."

"Oh, no," I said. I laughed and jumped up from the dressing table. "Rudy, I have to get to the Gaheimer House and get some work done, before Sylvia has a fit. And you know Sylvia having a fit is one of the scariest sights ever recorded by modern man."

"The kids are with your grandmother," he said with a mischievous grin. He came toward me, a growl starting low in his throat. When he gets like that, I may as well just give up. He grabbed me and kissed me on the neck, tickling my ribs in the process. I giggled and squirmed and he tickled all the more.

"Rudy! I mean it, I have to get some work . . . done. Stop it!" I yelled, but it did no good. All of my protestations turned into giggles and it's damn hard to take somebody seriously when they're giggling.

We landed on the bed, him on top. I wrestled a hand free and gave him some of his own medicine. I counted his ribs, up and down and up and down, until I thought he'd get sick from laughing. I love it when men are ticklish. It's so unmacho.

"You have the most gorgeous green eyes, mademoiselle," he said to me. I think he was trying to do a French accent, but somehow it sounded Hungarian. He jumped up off of the bed and took off running. I, of course, had to follow. He headed toward my office, which is the only other room upstairs, besides our bedroom and our bathroom. There we stood poised on the steps, him jabbing and I returning with jabs to his ribs. It was sort of like a sword fight without weapons. We circled each other, laughing.

I had the advantage. His back was to the steps.

"Okay, give up," I said. "I have the advantage. You've got nowhere to go. No retreat."

"Never!" he yelled. "Death first!" he shouted. He laughed wildly and pretended to lose his balance.

"If you think you'll scare me, you're sadly mistaken. I've been waiting for you to fall down a flight of stairs. That way I can be rid of you and it will be an accident," I said through laughter. I was joking and he knew it. This was something we did on a fairly regular basis.

This time it triggered something. Instead of the usual finale where we collapse on the bed, almost too tired for the sex we were playing at in the first place, I stopped.

"What?" he said at my sudden soberness.

"I can be rid of you and it will be an accident," I repeated, almost to myself. "It will *look* like an accident."

"What?" he asked. He followed me as I headed back into the bedroom.

"I'm beginning to wonder if Marie Dijon's death was really an accident."

"Oh, for Pete's sake!" he yelled. "You ruined my afternoon roll in the hay for that?" He was truly exasperated.

"I'm serious. She could have been pushed down those steps and nobody would ever know the difference."

"That includes you," he said.

I stuck my tongue out at him. I hate it when Rudy scores a point. "Okay, let me rephrase that. Nobody would know the difference, because nobody was looking for it. If I told the sheriff . . ."

"What?" he asked. "That you and your husband were tickling each other to death when you suddenly decided that Marie could have been pushed? Why? Why would somebody push her?"

"I don't know, but I just don't like the thought of somebody's life coming to an end because they tripped over their own house slipper or something."

"So you'd rather they be murdered? Oh, now that's a more comforting thought."

I suppose when put like that, it was rather ridiculous.

"All right, you win," I said. "But I do have to get to work."

"No."

"No, what?"

"I never win. Especially not that easily. You could keep arguing until the cows come home. What gives?" he asked.

"Nothing. You win," I said. "I was just being ridiculous."

•

I was seated at the desk of my office in the Gaheimer House on Jefferson Street. The New Kassel Historical Society office and general headquarters are located at the Gaheimer House. The president is one Sylvia Pershing. She's about ninety-four. Nobody knows her exact age because nobody has asked her. She will never die simply because she's too mean. It's one of those situations where God won't have her and hell is afraid she'll take over.

The vice president of the historical society is her sister Wilma, who is for the most part Sylvia's exact opposite. She's quiet, happy, and remarkably prudish. Neither have ever been married.

Sylvia now owns the Gaheimer House, one of several historic homes in our town built by an early settler named Hermann Gaheimer. I'm not sure what my role is exactly, because I have no title. But I give the tours, which I get paid for, and I take care of records and transcribe original documents in the archives and courthouses. I've even hired out my genealogical services and traced family trees, including my own.

The lineage we get is completely random, by the way. There's nothing grand or glorious, there's no divine reason that one person has a better family tree than the next. I am a descendant of a Revolutionary War soldier who was at Valley Forge. I can lay claim to the Dukes of Abercorn, and Robert the Bruce. I also have a private in the Union Army of the Civil War, and a Confederate private as well, so I suppose that means that I'm at war with myself. I even have an Indian, and no, she isn't a Cherokee princess.

I also have my share of deserters, illegitimates, and even a murderer. No kidding, I have an ancestor who beat his wife to death with a piece of firewood because his dinner wasn't cooked right. They lynched him. Finding out who I am was so much fun.

I'm basically of Scottish and French stock, with a little English thrown in for good measure. But the French is the blood that comes through the most. I'm short, with green eyes, and I tan easily. I did not, however, inherit my French ancestors' dark hair. Mine can't decide if it wants to be blond or brown and thus changes with the seasons.

Sylvia came into the office, glared at me, and sat down. I didn't think anything of it. Sylvia always glares at me.

"Yes, Sylvia, what can I do for you?"

"That Sheriff Brooke of yours has cornered the Dijon market."

"Wait," I said, holding up a hand. "First off, Sheriff Brooke is not mine. He's your great stepnephew. Secondly, what the heck is a Dijon market?"

Sylvia wears her hair in twisted braids on top of her head, just as Wilma does. She's very thin, has silver gray eyes and entirely too much energy for somebody sixty-something years my senior.

"Marie Dijon. There will be an estate sale, and I've heard the sheriff is going to make a bid for everything in the woman's house. Nobody else in New Kassel can counter that offer."

"Well, since he bought Norah's Antiques, he's been throwing everything he has into it. He's trying to set it up for his retirement," I explained. Sylvia said nothing. She could more than afford to counter any offer that Sheriff Brooke wanted to make. I happen to know personally that Hermann Gaheimer left Sylvia a million and something dollars when he died in the 1930s.

It is knowledge that I should not possess.

Sylvia was single-handedly responsible for renovating the town and had loaned many people money to start businesses, interest free. She could counter his offer if she wanted. But she didn't want to draw too much attention to just how much money she was sitting on. She even made the town hold fund-raisers for the historical society. Part of that was to cover up her wealth. The other was because she wanted the people of New Kassel to have to work for things. I understood that train of thought. Sylvia was such a complex person.

"Well, Sylvia," I began diplomatically, "if Sheriff Brooke wants to 'corner the market,' so to speak, he certainly has his inalienable rights."

"Oh, pooh," she said. She narrowed her gray eyes on me. "I know for a fact that Marie Dijon had some very rare and expensive pieces in her possession. I think that the people who have a little knowledge of antiques and a respect for historical items should be allowed to at least view what she had and have a chance to bid on them," she said. She was very serious.

It felt suddenly stuffy in the office. It is small and has only one window covered by a lace curtain. One wall has an antique rose of Sharon quilt hanging on it. It is a beautiful quilt with pink appliquéd roses and a swirling green vine. No matter how beautiful it is, it makes the room more confining. And Sylvia did not help my claustrophobia any.

"It will be some time before all the legal junk is finished and anybody can really make a serious offer. Sheriff Brooke is probably just blowing hot air," I said. "What do you want me to do about it?"

"Why, tell him he cannot do this, of course."

I laughed at her. I laughed heartily because I knew just how serious she was.

"Victory, you are treading on thin ice, young lady. You show me the respect that I deserve."

"Yes, Sylvia."

I tried to straighten up and act right. It was sort of like in the fifth grade when Miss Thomas told us all to "straighten up and fly right." It didn't work then because she had a long piece of toilet paper hanging out of the waistband of her pants. This didn't work either because I could just imagine me telling Sheriff Brooke that he wasn't allowed to bid on an estate. The vision it evoked brought me to laughing again. "I'm sorry, Sylvia. I'm trying."

"Marie Dijon was a very generous and giving woman," Sylvia said. "I don't think that she would want one stingy human being to get everything she had."

"What do you mean, *generous?*" I asked.

Sylvia looked uncomfortable. "Well, you know the earrings that you wear with the chenille-ball fringe dress?" she asked.

"Yes," I said. "The gold ones with pearl drops?"

"Those are the ones. Well, they were on loan from Marie."

"On loan?" I asked.

"Yes. She said to just pay her whenever, and I never paid her."

"You stole the earrings?" I asked, amazed.

"Of course not. They are very expensive. They are pre-revolutionary France. Something like seventeenth century."

"Oh, crap," I said.

"No vulgarities in the Gaheimer House, young lady."

"How expensive?" I asked. "Sylvia? How expensive?"

"At least twenty thousand."

"Dollars?!"

"Now you know why I hadn't gotten around to paying her for them. I intended to, but then she died."

I thought about this for a minute. "So, in other words, since the earrings aren't paid for, you have to return them to the estate, to be auctioned off."

"If I want to be honest about it. I could keep them and nobody would ever know the difference, but I won't do that. I have to be honest about it. But I'd like to keep them in the Gaheimer collection, and I can't if Sheriff Brooke buys the entire estate."

"Twenty thousand," I repeated.

"They are rumored to have been worn by Anne of Austria."

"Well, that's one expensive rumor."

"Do you know who Anne of Austria was?" Sylvia asked me.

"Yes, the wife of Louis the . . . uh—I hate Roman numbers—the thirteenth," I said.

"Yes. I'm impressed," she said.

"I'm sure if you ask Sheriff Brooke, he'd be happy to make a settlement over the earrings."

"I want you to do it. I refuse to speak with him," she said and arose from her chair. "There are a few things in the top drawer that need to be returned to her estate, as well as the earrings. Please see to it that Mr. Reaves receives them. I will keep the earrings in my safety deposit box until an agreement can be met."

"How do you know that Mr. Reaves is handling her estate?"

"Victory, there's very little that goes on in this town that I don't know about," she said and then added, "Bernice Thorley told me."

She was out of my office as fast as she had come in.

I picked up the telephone and called the law office of Wilbert Reaves. A young, feminine voice answered the phone.

"Wilbert Reaves, attorney at law," Jamie said.

"Hello, Jamie. This is Torie O'Shea. I need to speak with Wilbert."

"He's not here. Won't be for the rest of the day."

"Well, can you see when he has an opening? I need to bring

him some things and speak to him regarding the Marie Dijon will."

"Tomorrow around two, or you can catch him out at the Dijon place this evening. I'm pretty sure he said that he'd be out there around seven this evening."

"All right. I'll try that. Thank you."

Three

After dinner, I read the kids a story, then did the dishes. My oldest daughter, Rachel, is seven now, and even though she can read, she likes it when I read stories to her. She has brownish hair and extraordinary black eyes, and Rudy is already concerned about how he is going to fight off the hormone-pumped teenage boys. My youngest daughter, Mary, is three, almost four. She has blond hair and green eyes and is slightly more plump than Rachel. She will not sit still for anything in this world, except *Aladdin* and my story time.

My mother was at her sister's house in Meyersville, visiting my grandmother. My mother is the youngest of four daughters, three of whom live within ten miles of New Kassel. Aunt Millicent lives in West Virginia.

Rudy was late getting in, so I had to take the kids with me to meet Mr. Reaves. I decided that I'd walk down to Marie's house instead of taking the car. It takes more gas starting the darn thing than it does to get two blocks down the road. From about ten in the morning to five in the evening the streets are usually packed with tourists. This late in the evening, the only tourists out were the ones going to dinner or staying at the Murdoch Inn.

There was nobody at Marie's house when the children and I arrived at quarter till seven. I sat on the front porch of her house, watching the birds pecking at the ground in her front yard. I could see the very top of my roof from Marie's porch.

I played with the envelope awhile, wondering why Sylvia insisted upon me returning this to Mr. Reaves. All the envelope contained was Marie's family tree and a minor history of the Dijon family. Usually, we keep that sort of thing on file or at least make copies. But Sylvia had insisted that I return it.

So, there I sat, waiting for Mr. Reaves. Now that I thought about it, I couldn't figure out why he'd be coming to Marie's house in the first place unless he was meeting an individual about her will. Or maybe a contester? Oooh, now that would be a bit of juicy gossip.

Directly across, the firehouse was quiet, as it usually was. We had three firemen, plus our chief, and six volunteer firemen. There was usually only one person at the firehouse at a time, other than the fire chief, Elmer Kolbe, who seemed to live there. He happened to be out front at the moment. He washed the red fire truck, taking particular care around the headlights, as if it were a human being. I waved to him, and he waved back.

I was bored. Which is when bad things usually happen.

I suddenly realized that the girls were no longer on the front porch. I could hear their giggling voices coming from the backyard. I walked around the back of the house by way of the driveway.

Both girls were hopping like bunny rabbits in the recently loosened dirt of Marie's flower bed. Wherever Rachel hopped, Mary hopped, but with much more effort because her legs were a great deal shorter. Their pigtails flopped on top of their heads with every jump they made.

"Girls, get out of the flower bed," I said, vaguely even remembering that they were actually in the flower bed. I was too interested in looking at the back of Marie's house. There was no crime scene tape or anything, because there was no crime scene. The sheriff's department had collected everything they wanted within the first two days of her accident. Nobody had been here in two or three days at least.

I'm not sure what it was I was looking for, only that I was looking for something. Anything that seemed out of place.

Just then, I saw a flash of purple. One of my girls was climbing on the back porch banisters. Which one was it? They were dressed in matching purple short outfits, purple with little orange squiggly things.

"Rachel! Get down."

"It isn't me, Mom. I'm over here."

Rachel was still in the flower bed. I had assumed that it was her climbing on the banisters because she was the oldest. Oldest doesn't automatically make her the bravest, I suppose. "I told you five minutes ago to get out of that flower bed. Why don't you listen to me? Your sister listened to me," I said.

True. But she was hanging upside down on a banister at the moment, ready to drop on her head from seven feet.

"Mary! Get down. No, don't get down. I'll come and get you," I said. I realized in midsentence that it would be like her just to jump. "Rachel, come with me. Now. You probably trampled those poor flowers to death. Not to mention what you've got all over your new white tennis shoes." Why are they always *new* white tennis shoes? They are never old white tennis shoes. I suppose because if they were old they wouldn't be white anymore. I don't know why all of the marketing geniuses can't invent brown tennis shoes and just get it over with.

When I finally reached the back porch, I grabbed Mary off the banister by her feet. She put her hands on the floor of the porch and then flipped over. I shook my finger at her. "This is not our house. You can't just destroy other people's property."

Not that she was free to destroy ours either.

I stood on my tiptoes and peeked in Marie's back door. I leaned a little too hard on the door, and it swung open with a creak.

An open door is the worst temptation. It's worse than chocolate. I tried convincing myself that what I really wanted to do was okay. After all, I'd have to step inside the kitchen in order to reach the door to shut it, right?

I should have been a lawyer.

Just then, Mary took off and was inside Marie's house before I could stop her. All right, somewhere deep down I knew that I shouldn't do it. But what if the sheriff missed something? They were so intent on it being an accident, I don't think they wanted to look at it as a possible crime scene.

"Come on, Rachel," I said to her. She came in behind me. I grabbed Mary by the hand and set the envelope that I had been holding on the kitchen table.

"Mary, don't touch anything. You touch anything and you won't play on the swing set for a year. Understood?" She nodded.

I started to turn on the light and then stopped myself. The electricity was probably still on, but I didn't want to bring attention to the fact that somebody was in her house. I suppose that impulse was sort of a confession that I knew I shouldn't have been in there in the first place.

The sun had set, but I could still see. There was at least twenty minutes of twilight before dusk set in and then it would be too dark to see.

Everything looked as if she'd just went out to the store and would be right back. There were dishes in the drain, along with two glasses on the table and a jug of milk. I opened the refrigerator and was nearly knocked over by the bright light it shone. I shut it quickly, noting that the inside of her refrigerator looked as normal as the inside of mine. It had been five days since she'd died. She had lain at the foot of the steps for nearly two days before Ransford had found her.

A foul odor crept from the trash bin, and I wondered how bad that milk on the table would smell if I took the lid off. Why hadn't the sheriff's department poured it down the drain and taken out the trash? This was gross.

"Mom," Rachel said in her usual condescending tone when she was about to bawl me out for something. "What are we doing in here?"

"Looking."

"Looking at what? There aren't any lights on. Mom, why are we walking around in the dark?"

"The electricity is off," I said. I hoped that would be a good enough answer for a while.

"Nuh uh," she said. "The 'frigerator is on."

You pray that you have really intelligent children all of your life. Then when you do, they end up being too smart for you.

"Hush up, Rachel. Okay? I'm not going to stand here in the dark and argue as to why I'm doing whatever it is I'm doing. If I want to walk through this house in the dark, I will. And you aren't old enough to question me as to why. All right? Are we clear on this, girls? Mary, you touch nothing. Rachel, you say nothing. Once we get out of here, you can ask me all the questions you want to."

Rachel sighed.

I walked through the rest of the house, holding Mary's hand tightly so she couldn't get away, and I noticed that the house was indeed done in expensive taste, from what I could see. The furniture was all antique. China and fluted crystal were set everywhere. I couldn't make out specific details, like color schemes, since it was so dark. Her bedroom was neat and orderly, the covers on one side of the bed turned down, looking as though it had been slept in, if only for an hour. The bed did not give the appearance of being messed up enough for an entire night's sleep.

Marie got up in the middle of the night, went to the kitchen for a glass of milk, and for some reason decided to go into the basement? That didn't make sense. I know I only go in my basement at high noon.

Of course, I'm also a chicken. Maybe Marie was not as frightened of things that go bump in the night as I am.

But an older woman who lived alone? Why go to the basement?

There was something dark lying on her bed. I looked closer. It was a hairbrush.

"Mommy," Mary said. "I have to go pee."

I headed back through the living room for the kitchen, and stopped at the basement door. Opening it, I wasn't the least bit disappointed by the fact that it was dark and icky smelling. I hadn't expected anything else.

"I am *not* going down there," Rachel said. "No way. Forget it."

Bending down on one knee, I examined the floor near the first step. There was no raised piece of tile or anything. No nail sticking up to cause her to trip. I stood up.

"So she just stood here and fell," I said aloud. She had on a housecoat that came to her knees, so that wasn't long enough to interfere with her walking. And she had on house slippers.

I have to admit, those can be difficult to walk in.

Bright headlights appeared in Marie's kitchen window.

The lights cast sharp angular shadows of the knickknacks sitting around. Rachel gasped and I slammed the basement door shut and prepared to run outside. Only, I heard the car door shut. The lights were still shining inside, on high beam.

"Shoot."

"Mommy, I gotta go pee," Mary said.

I slumped to the floor, and instantly felt ridiculous for doing so, especially since both of my children were still standing up looking down at me with superior amusement.

What if it was Mr. Reaves coming to meet whomever it was that he was supposed to meet? I might be able to explain being in the house, but I'd never be able to explain being on the floor.

"Mom, it's a car," Rachel said.

Just as I was about to get up, the doorknob turned. I could see a vague outline of a man. He had a cigarette hanging out of his mouth, smoke distorting the glass. It could not be Mr. Reaves. The man standing on the other side of the door was way too tall.

So why didn't he come in? He knew the door was unlocked.

Unlike me, he probably had respect for private property.

So, there I sat on Marie Dijon's kitchen floor, looking up at the underneath side of her kitchen table. Thanks to the bright headlights, it was an enlightening position. Silver duct tape held a fat manila envelope onto the underneath side of the table. Money? Jewelry? Something that Marie Dijon did not want anybody to find.

"Mom?"

"Get down," I said to them. The man walked away from the door, but I did not hear him get back in the car. I crawled to the bathroom.

"Okay, Mary, you pee. Rachel, you watch her and make sure

she pees. Don't come out of this bathroom unless I say to. And don't make any noise."

"Well, Mom. You know, Mary has to make noise when she goes pee."

"Okay. No noise after she's done going. Okay?"

I crawled into the living room to try to get a better look at the car. Standing up, I tried to flatten my body against the living-room wall to look out. I barely moved the dotted swiss curtains. It was nearly dusk now, and all I could make out was that the car was not huge, but it wasn't compact either, and that it was a dark color. Well, that ought to cover at least half of the cars in New Kassel.

Then I saw the back of the man's head as he walked underneath the window. Somehow, I got the weirdest feeling that he knew I was in the house.

It all seemed to fit perfectly then. Marie Dijon had been asleep the night she died. She heard a knock at the door, which would account for why there was no forced entry. She brushed her hair, left the brush on the bed, put on house slippers and a housecoat. Whoever she let in, she knew fairly well. She got out the milk and two glasses, but never got to pour the milk.

Why would she go to the basement steps? That made no sense.

Finally, the man outside the window got back in the car and left. I ran full speed into the kitchen, stepped on something in the hallway that threw off my balance, and my stomach and ribs met the floor with a thud.

"Ugh," was all I managed.

I got up slowly and cautiously, and went to the kitchen table. I grabbed the envelope that I had brought with me off of the kitchen table. It only took me a second to talk myself into my next move. I reached down and tore off the envelope that was taped underneath her table, it making a *shwishk* sound in the process.

"Girls, let's go!" I shouted. I met them at the living-room entryway, and then we were out the door with both envelopes in two seconds and home in five minutes.

NEW KASSEL GAZETTE

THE NEWS YOU MIGHT MISS
by Eleanore Murdoch

It's apple pickin' time! Volunteers are needed up at the orchard this year more than ever since Wilma Pershing's apple butter has become famous. She received a fan letter from a U.S. senator on her wonderful apple butter, stating that it was actually better than his mother's. This year's contest is for the best apple dumpling recipe.

And thank you to everybody who wrote in praise of my new society column that made its debut a few months ago. New Kassel readers say they feel more informed than ever about life in their town. I'm just glad to be able to bring it to you.

We're taking up a collection to buy Tobias a new accordion. Donations can be made at Fraulein Krista's.

Until next time.

Eleanore

Four

Cautious is not a word I would use to describe myself, unless it deals with my children or germs. Then I'm usually overly cautious to the point of complete paranoia. But in my endeavors that don't include the girls or communicable bacteria, I tend to jump in with both feet before I've thought anything through. I usually end up in hot water up to my neck.

The envelope that I had so illegally obtained from Marie Dijon's house contained a key. It also contained some documents that were very old and very French. The next day, I took my French/English dictionary and went down to Fräulein Krista's restaurant to try to decipher them and stuff my face with raspberry turnovers in the process. Work is the ideal excuse to eat.

Fräulein Krista's Speisehaus is one of my favorite places to eat. It is directly across the street from the Gaheimer House, with the Christmas Shop on one side and the rectory of Santa Lucia on the other. The waiters wear green velvet knickers and the waitresses green velvet dresses, resembling adult Hansels and Gretels. The place reminded me of an inn deep in the Bavarian Alps.

Two hours later I had a headache the size of Montana, not

to mention a guilty conscience, and only a few words here and there that made any sense. I decided that I needed a French translator.

Camille Lombarde was such a person. She lived up in St. Louis, and I decided that I would go to see her one day this week.

"You look as though you are halfway around the world," a voice said to me. I glanced up and Krista Dougherty, the owner of this fine establishment, was smiling down at me from her lofty five-feet-eleven.

"I am," I answered her. "I'm in France."

She pulled out the chair across from me and sat down. If you were expecting a textbook specimen of the Aryan race to own Fräulein Krista's, you won't be disappointed. Krista had ocean blue eyes, dimples, freckles, and natural blond hair, and as I pointed out just before, she is very tall.

"Well, say hello for me to a wonderful artist I met there four summers ago. His name was Christophe." She smiled at the memory.

"I wish I could, because then I wouldn't need to hunt down a translator. I could ask anybody on the street."

"Oh," she said. "Working on something for Sylvia?"

"No, this one is just for me," I said. I couldn't very well spread the news that these were illegally obtained documents from Marie's house. I tried to put them back in the envelope as nonchalantly as I could.

"Just as well, I suppose."

"That's an odd thing to say," I said. "What do you mean by it?"

Looking at me peculiarly she said, "Have you read today's paper?"

"No. Should I have?"

She picked at her nails, and genuinely looked as though she didn't want to be the bearer of bad news. "Well, it seems that Eleanore Murdoch—"

"Say no more," I said with my hand in the air. "I've been having trouble with that woman all summer. What has she written now? That Sylvia is having an affair with the sheriff, for Pete's sake?"

Krista was not smiling.

"What?" I asked. "Oh, come on. What could Eleanore possibly know that could be that bad? Most everything she prints is an exaggeration anyway."

"I'm sure this is an exaggeration," she said. "But nevertheless, people get things in their head . . ."

"What? What? Krista, just tell me what it is right now or . . . or I'll dunk your golden locks into a jar of maple syrup!"

A bubble of contagious laughter spilled from her. "So how many chickens do you and Rudy have now?"

"About two dozen."

"And only one rooster?"

"Yes, well, he's a very happy rooster. Quit changing the subject, Krista."

"Well, I was thinking that we could strike up a contract. You supply me with eggs every morning for the breakfasts, and I'll pay you."

"Krista!" I said, my patience running out.

"Well, I guess it won't hurt, since you can read it anywhere. It seems that Eleanore has accused Sylvia of murder."

I laughed. I belly laughed. "That's the most preposterous thing I've ever heard," I said. "Sylvia is a lot of things, but no murderer," I defended her. "Pray tell, who has she murdered?"

"Sophie Gaheimer."

"Hermann Gaheimer's wife? Well, that woman died more than seventy years ago."

"Yes, and Eleanore claims that Sophie committed suicide as a direct result of an illicit love affair between Hermann and Sylvia," Krista said. "Thus holding Sylvia responsible."

The smile left my face. Not long ago, I discovered the will of Hermann Gaheimer that Sylvia had locked up in a cabinet downstairs in the basement of the Gaheimer House. In it, Hermann left everything to his "beloved Sylvia." At the time, Hermann was ninety-one or so years old, and Sylvia was but thirty. I had found it strange then that he willed only a small cash settlement to the children he had with Sophie, and instead left everything to Sylvia, but I kept it to myself.

Sylvia knew that I'd been in the drawer, but I told her that I saw nothing of importance in the file cabinet, and we haven't spoken of it again.

"Torie," Krista said, "you don't look so well. Have I upset you?"

"No. *You* haven't upset me. Life upsets me."

"Well, if it's any consolation to you, I thought it was rude and very petty," Krista said. "For Eleanore to print something like that—I mean, I have no great love for Sylvia, but that was rude."

"Yes, it was," I said. "Well, I guess I better head on over and find out if she's read the paper. That way I can get home and nurse my wounds and be healed by the time my family comes strolling home for the day."

I crossed the street, head down, aiming for the Gaheimer House and wondering how in the heck one itty-bitty town could have so many problems. The Gaheimer House is large, three stories, and sits right on the sidewalk. On really hot days, you can feel the heat coming from the red brick of the building just walking by it. It is a burnt-red color. The windowsills are a cream color and surrounded by forest green shutters. It's not a pretty combination but I'm not about to tell Sylvia.

I entered the foyer and made my way through the living room, which is decorated in almost entirely Victorian furniture, laces, and doohickeys. Some decorating genius decided that if you had a spare inch in your home during the Victorian era, you had to cover it. That genius was Queen Victoria herself, actually.

The furniture is covered in an emerald green and blackberry paisley. It looks quite nice, especially set against the original oak floor.

I went through the ballroom, the hall, and finally my office. I set the envelope down on my desk and went to find Sylvia or Wilma. One of them was always around, even though they did not live here.

"Sylvia?"

I heard her determined footsteps as she came from the kitchen. "Yes, what is it?"

She was collected and poised. If she'd read the paper, she showed no outward signs of it. But that was Sylvia. "What do you want, Victory?"

"Did you know that Marie Dijon was descended from Charlemagne?" When in doubt on how to approach a subject, don't.

"I thought I told you to return those papers to the estate. Did I or did I not?"

Sylvia Pershing is the only woman in the entire world who can fluster me to the point that all my language skills fly out the window. Something wasn't right. Sylvia wasn't right.

"I did. I mean, you did. And I tried to, but Mr. Reaves wasn't where he was supposed to be last night, so I thought I'd take a closer look at the papers."

"That's the very thing that seems to get you into trouble," she said. She turned and stomped off down the hallway and into the kitchen. I felt very stupid standing in the hallway just outside of my office, alone. So, I followed her.

"I'm serious, Sylvia. On her father's side she was descended from Charlemagne, who in turn was descended from three hundred years of Merovingian kings all the way back to Pharamond. On her mother's side she was descended from Hengist the Saxon. Do you know who Hengist the Saxon is? Or was, I should say. I do. I'm probably one of the few people that somebody could walk up to and say, 'Hey, do you know who Hengist the Saxon was?' and I'd be able to say yes."

"Is there a point to this?" Sylvia asked me, her head shaking slightly from age and irritation.

"Well no, not really. It's just that when I was a teenager, I hated the time and place that I lived in so much that I spent all my time in 450 A.D. And thus, I know who Hengist the Saxon was."

"And? Who was he?"

"Oh, just some Prince of Jutes. And King of Kent, around 457 or so. He defeated the Britons several times, and he is also a descendant of Woden."

"Woden?"

"Yes, largely mythical. Sort of like . . . King Arthur. Except Woden was the ancestor of Cerdic the Saxon who was in turn an ancestor to Alfred the Great."

"Aah," she said. "Finally a name that I recognize. Once more, Victory, is there a point to all of this?"

My palms were sweating, and I was suddenly very nervous. "Well, no. But Marie's father's line, the French one, it's very interesting indeed. See, she's descended from the Charlemagne line through Louis IV, through his son Charles, Duke of Lorraine."

"Yes."

"Her family were the rightful heirs to the French throne when Louis V died in 987. If the crown had gone to the correct bloodline, there would never have been an Anne of Austria or Louis XIV, or the dauphin held prisoner during the French Revolution. There may not have ever been a revolution. Hugh Capet came along and usurped the throne, on a claim through his mother's line. She was a descendant of Charlemagne as well, only through his son Pepin, the King of Italy. Hugh had no real male claim. His father had been the son-in-law of Louis I. Son-in-law is not a strong enough claim to a throne when there are direct male descendants of the king."

She did not respond for a moment. "Are you feeling okay?" she asked me. "Why the excitement over a lineage? You've seen lineages of this caliber before."

"Well, sure. But very few have lived in New Kassel, and I was wondering why you wished to return the documents instead of copying them and displaying them, like you did mine?"

"You are descended from Robert the Bruce. He was a great man."

"As was Charlemagne. Besides, Robert the Bruce is descended from Charlemagne. Every royal household was descended from Charlemagne in one form or other."

"Well," Sylvia said, "then what's all the hooplala over Marie's lineage?"

"Well, like most Americans, our lineage bleeds out into lowly knights, seneschals, grooms-of-the-bedchamber—those types of titles, or eventually individuals with no title or land and so they come to America. But Marie's line was titled clear up to the revolution in France."

"Interesting."

"Yes, and I was wondering why you didn't see fit to keep this lineage for our records, like we usually do."

She looked out the window. "No reason."

"Sylvia, what's the matter?"

"Nothing."

"Bull. What is it?" I asked.

"If you must know," she said, spinning around to face me. "I have always liked to believe that you and I had a professional respect for each other."

"I'd like to think that, too," I said.

"You have betrayed me." It was not hurt that I saw in her eyes, it was anger.

"I what? What have I done?" I was genuinely surprised.

"I know that you told Eleanore Murdoch about . . ."

"No, Sylvia—"

She held a hand up for me to stop talking, which I did. I always listen to Sylvia. She is a great authority figure. I never could understand where that authority came from.

"Now, everything has been undone. All my hard work."

"Sylvia, I did not tell Eleanore about the will or anything. I swear to you. You know she has access to newspapers and the courthouse the same as you or I. All she had to do was look it up."

"How did she know about Sophie?"

I stared in disbelief. My mind wasn't comprehending what it was that she was saying to me. "What do you mean? You mean Sophie really did commit suicide?"

"Yes," she said and hung her head.

"Jesus Christ," I mumbled. She started to protest my vulgarities in the Gaheimer House and I stopped her. "Jesus Christ is not a vulgarity. I was appealing to him."

"You're a clever woman, Victory."

"Look, Sylvia. I swear to you that I said nothing to Eleanore. I wouldn't give her my grocery list. So far as Sophie's suicide, I can't tell you where she got the information, unless it was in the papers as well."

"No," Sylvia answered me. "It wasn't. It was kept out because of their children and grandchildren."

"When did she commit suicide?"

"1922," she said. "I was nineteen."

I suddenly felt sorry for Sylvia. I was trying to imagine what it must have been like to be nineteen and to have to live the next seventy-odd years thinking that you were indirectly responsible for your lover's wife's suicide. I had no words to give her.

"You don't think that Eleanore just took a guess and got it right?"

"No. I think not."

"Oh, Sylvia. I am truly sorry."

"Don't be," she said. She straightened her shoulders. "I have wrongly accused you. Forgive me," she said and waltzed past me as stately as ever.

Five

When I arrived home, my mother was cooking dinner. She is fifty-two and still a very beautiful woman. She has an oval face with creamy skin and dark brown eyes. She has a certain regal air to her, as though she'd been to the finest finishing school in New York. In reality she had not finished high school, thanks to polio. When she became confined to a wheelchair some forty-three years ago, there was no way to get to school. In the fifties there was no transportation for the disabled in Huntington, West Virginia, and her mother and father both worked long hours.

"Hey, Mom. What's up?"

"Not much. Rudy called and said he's going to have to go to Indianapolis in the morning. The only flight he could get is four in the morning. So he wants to know if you'd pack his suitcase for him, so he can go right to bed when he gets in?"

"Sure, no problem."

I turned to head out to the back porch but was stopped by Sheriff Brooke standing in the doorway. He had a rather determined look on his face.

"Oh, hello, Sheriff. I didn't know you were coming for dinner."

He crossed his arms and raised an eyebrow.

"Mmm-mmm. Smell that corn bread?" I asked. "Fried potatoes, too. Well, lucky you."

Just then, Rachel came in through the back door, scrambled between his legs, and came to me. "Hi, Mom."

"Hello, sweetie," I said and hugged her.

"Rachel and I just had a very interesting conversation," Sheriff Brooke said.

"Really? Well, she's a fairly interesting kid."

"Yes," he said as he walked toward me. I instinctively backed up. He pulled out a chair and sat down at the kitchen table. "I can't wait to hear your explanation for the outrageous events she told me about."

"Well, you know seven-year-olds. They have the greatest imaginations."

"What were you doing in Marie Dijon's house?" he asked me.

I wiped my sweaty palms on my jeans and wondered how I would get out of this one. My mother turned to me then from the stove looking very maternal. Not maternal-pity, but maternal-angry.

"I can get you for breaking and entering, and don't think because you are Jalena's daughter that I won't do it, because I will."

"Only entering. I didn't break in."

"God!" he said. "You had your children with you!"

"It's not what it seems."

"Oh, I'm waiting," he said as he clasped his hands behind his head. "Your explanations are always the best in the world."

"I went out there to return some documents to Mr. Reaves."

"Why there?" he asked. "That makes no sense."

"I had some documents that were Marie Dijon's. Sylvia

wanted me to return them. When I called his office, Jamie said he wouldn't be in for the rest of the day, but that I could catch him over at Marie's around seven. I went over there, only he never showed up," I said. "Jeez, I wouldn't have taken my children if I had gone over there intending to snoop. What kind of mother do you think I am? Don't answer that question."

Mother wheeled over to the table and placed a large platter of fried catfish on the table. She stared at me for a few seconds, letting me know with eye contact only that I hadn't heard from her yet over this matter.

"So how did you get inside?"

"The door was open. Mary ran inside."

"So you couldn't turn around and walk back out?"

I couldn't answer that question. At least not without condemning myself.

"Why didn't you turn on the lights?" he asked.

He was on a roll.

"Because you didn't want anybody to know that you were in there," he said. "Isn't that right?"

"Rachel, go in your room and play," I said.

"But, Mom—"

"You're not in trouble. Just go on and play."

She left, reluctantly.

"Rachel said that you shut them in the bathroom," Sheriff Brooke said.

"Wait. Hold everything. Mary had to go to the bathroom, and I'm not answering any more of these questions until you've answered a few of mine."

"I don't have to answer your questions," he said.

"Then you can get out of my house."

My mother said nothing. I knew she wouldn't interrupt.

This fight was between me and the sheriff. My mother was one of the most incredibly fair individuals I have ever known. I think it is something she learned from spending a lifetime in a wheelchair. She has observed more situations than most people.

"What? What do you want to know?" he asked.

"I'd like to know why this was not investigated as a homicide," I said.

"There is no reason for it to be. Duran checked out the scene. He questioned people. There is no reason to believe that her death was anything but an accident. I read the report."

"I'm not saying that somebody killed her on purpose. It could have been the result of an argument that went too far."

"Where's your evidence?" he asked me. "There is no reason to believe that there was even another person in the house."

"Okay," I said, "listen to this theory. And listen with an open mind."

He gave me a snarl, which in his heathen way meant that he would try to listen objectively. Oscar the Grouch has nothing on this guy. He waited with minimal patience as I tried to formulate in my mind what it was I wanted to say. Even my mother had stopped slicing tomatoes to listen to what I was about to tell him.

I cleared my throat. "She lives alone. Just like you, Sheriff. You live alone. If you get up in the middle of the night to get a drink or go to the bathroom, do you bother with a housecoat? Slippers? I could see the slippers if it's the dead of winter. But it's September. I happen to know that the night Marie died it was sixty-seven degrees at two in the morning, because I called the weather bureau and found out. Now," I said, swallowing, "let's go a step further. Would you bother brushing your hair? If you were going to get a drink in the kitchen by yourself at two in the morning, would you bother with a housecoat, slippers, and brushing your hair to get a glass of milk?"

He said nothing.

My mother spoke up then. "In the middle of the night, I wouldn't bother with it, and I don't live alone. I wouldn't expect to run into anybody in the kitchen. But even if I did bother with the housecoat and slippers, I definitely wouldn't brush my hair."

"And neither would most people," I added.

Sheriff Brooke still said nothing.

"Well?" I asked.

"I might agree with you on that. But how do you know that's what happened?" he asked.

"It's been established by forensics that the time of death was sometime between eleven P.M. and four A.M. on Wednesday morning, and don't ask me how I found out that information because I will not tell you." The sheriff rolled his eyes heavenward. I don't know if that was in frustration, aggravation, or exasperation. Probably all three. I continued. "Anyway, I found a hairbrush on the foot of her bed, like she'd brushed her hair before she got up to answer the door. Everybody knows that she had on slippers and a robe. But this is the kicker. There were two clean glasses sitting on her table next to the jug of milk."

His face changed expressions completely. He sat to attention then. "You're sure?"

"Yes. Why would she get out two glasses? I think that somebody knocked at her door, so she brushed her hair, put on the robe, and so forth. *She let in her killer*. Whether or not the person came there with the intent to kill her, or if it was a result of an argument, I don't know. But she was not alone," I said. "I don't think that she would have got out the milk before she

45

went to bed and forgot to put it away. And why the two glasses? There should have been only one," I said with great satisfaction.

Sheriff Brooke sat with one leg crossed over the other, picking at the heel of his boot. His eyebrows were knitted together. He was off in police land trying to piece together everything I'd just said.

"So," I said. "I ask you one more time. Why is this not being handled as a homicide?"

"Well, I left the crime scene. It was my day off and I thought Duran had it under control. I'll check into it, but that still doesn't take away from the fact that you were where you weren't supposed to be. With your children, no less!"

Sheriff Brooke stood up then and headed out to my back porch, stopping at the door. "I don't want to hear of you being on that property again. Do I make myself clear?"

"Yes, sir!" I said as I saluted him.

I was so thrilled with myself for convincing the sheriff that some pretty sloppy investigative work had been done that I forgot that my mother was still in the room. I was smiling to myself, like a schoolgirl who beat the smartest boy in the class in the math races. My smile soon faded as I looked into my mother's eyes.

"It was an accident," I pleaded. "I would not intentionally endanger my children."

She said nothing. I glanced out my back door and thought about Sheriff Brooke sitting out on my porch swing. I supposed that this would not be a good time to bring up the subject of his informal bid on Marie Dijon's estate.

Six

Camille Lombarde lived in an area of St. Louis known as the Central West End. It was an artsy neighborhood where one could find organic grocery stores, outdoor cafés, beautiful globed streetlights, cobblestoned streets and sidewalks, and every type of esoteric bookstore and music store imaginable. My favorite Chinese restaurant is located at the corner of Maryland and Euclid. The Magic Wok can't be beat for their lunchtime buffet.

The residences were old, pretty, and rich in architectural extravagance. Camille's residence was no different. Her house was, at one time, a building with several residences in it.

She bought the building, gutted it except for the original wood molding and wood floors, and made it one very large, enviable piece of property. It even had a courtyard with fountains and statues, all surrounded by a brick wall that was about eight feet tall, over which vines of every sort climbed.

I was seated in the courtyard somewhere in between a statue of the Venus de Milo and a fountain of a cherub with water squirting out of some fairly ingenious places. Camille, seated next to me, was a native of France, although she hadn't lived there in at least forty years. She had taught French at one of the universities in Atlanta for nearly thirty years and then retired to St. Louis.

I had gotten her name and address from Marie Dijon a while back. I had French documents from my family tree that I needed translated, and Marie said Camille would translate for twenty dollars an hour. Eventually Camille and I became friends, and we get together every now and then for lunch for the sheer enjoyment of each other's company.

"Torie," she began. "I would think by now that you had found the majority of your French ancestors."

She barely had an accent anymore, but it was still lingering in her *r*'s, especially when she got angry or excited. She was very wrinkled for her age, about sixty. She was also very charming, as I tend to think most Europeans are. Gray hair framed Camille's dark eyes and she was blessed with a small pert nose.

"This isn't for my family tree. These documents were . . . found in an old bureau that a friend of mine bought at an auction. They're very old. I made out the date on one of them to be April 1756."

Her eyebrows shot up on that one. I handed her the envelope.

"I don't know if they are written by anybody famous or worth any money, but we are very interested to hear what somebody from 1756 had to say."

"Well, I should say so. I am interested myself," she said. She carefully took the papers out of the envelope.

"I managed to make out a few things. One of them is written to a countess, but no name is given, only her title."

"Let's take these into my office. It looks like rain, no?"

Yes, it did look like rain. Dark clouds were moving in from the west at a fairly fast pace. A slight wind kicked up some leaves around the patio.

I didn't have to tell her that she held photocopies. She could tell that the paper was not old. It had taken me hours to copy them because the papers were so fragile and I was afraid that they would get torn.

"Maybe you have found the correspondence of a dangerous *liaison,*" she said with a smile.

We entered her den, which looked like something right out of a French château; vanilla-colored walls with dark cherry trim, large settees everywhere, and a marble fireplace were the highlights of the room. The den included bookshelves that went from floor to ceiling on two walls. I found this quite impressive because she had twelve-foot ceilings. She had a table set up in the middle of the room, complete with fluorescent lamps and magnifiers.

She sat down, grabbed her glasses from the end of the table, and began scanning the papers. "Get me a piece of paper from my desk," she said without looking up. "And a pencil."

I obliged. After a few minutes she looked up at me, with a disturbed look on her face. "Torie, I may need a few days to work on these."

"What's wrong?"

"Nothing's wrong. I just think they are going to be a little difficult to translate. They are in two-hundred-and-fifty-year-old French. The handwriting is not that great."

I suppose I didn't look completely convinced.

"At the least it's going to take me twelve hours. Do you have twelve hours to sit in my den and watch me?"

"Well, no. But . . . well, not to insult you, Camille, but I'm not real thrilled about—"

"Leaving them with me."

"No. It's not you. I'm just really impatient. Not to mention generally paranoid. It has nothing to do with you."

"Well, some of them may never be translated."

"Why?"

"Look at this one," she said. "It's nothing but numbers."

"Like an accounting report or something?"

"No. It's in a code."

The implications of that rocked me to my feet. In code? What in the heck had I found? What the heck did Marie Dijon have? I swallowed nervously.

"It would have to be decoded first, and then translated. But here's the tricky part. The numbers are written in French, as in *quatre onze vingt*. But who's to say that the words that they spell out will be in French? They could spell out words in English, Dutch, Russian. Any number of languages and even then the words could be purely allegorical. It just depends on how far the author tried to go to keep this information safe."

I felt the blood run from my face. Surely if it was something from the 1700s it wouldn't be pertinent to this century's events.

"Of course, who's to say they are even authentic? Whatever they say will have to be authenticated. You know, the originals will have to be dated?" she said. That was the only indication she gave that she was aware I had the originals elsewhere. They were in my safety deposit box, to which only Rudy and I had keys.

"Yes, I know."

"Even if they are dated at the eighteenth century, the author could have been writing a novel, or could have written false truths. It doesn't mean anything."

Why was she trying so hard to convince me? She had barely glanced at the documents and yet she was acting as if she already knew that they contained earthshaking news. I didn't feel as though I could leave these documents with her. And yet, if I didn't? Who could I get to translate them without putting me in debt? I didn't know anybody else.

"I'm not all that concerned about their value or authenticity," I said. "I was just curious as to what they said."

"I will keep them in my safe. Yes? Will that make you feel better?"

No, not really. But it's not like they were the originals. Right? I suppose in my paranoid head I just had this awful feeling that the copies would be destroyed by a spilled cup of coffee or something equally bizarre, and then my originals would burn in a fire and then I'd never know what they said. Is that not the working of a truly paranoid mind?

"Of course," I said. "I'll pick them up, say tomorrow around three?"

"That should give me plenty of time. I don't really have much else to do. I will give them my full attention. And I'll take good care of them."

"I know you will. Call me if you need anything."

•

I kicked the soda machine that was located in the hall outside of my office, an hour after I had left Camille. A Dr Pepper costs fifty cents. So, for some reason, this machine will not give me a Dr Pepper unless I put in sixty cents or more. It's like it forgets that I already gave it a dime. Sylvia got the proceeds from the machine, though. That should tell me something.

I went back into my little claustrophobic office and found Eleanore Murdoch seated in the chair across from mine. She didn't hide the fact that she was reading the documents on my desk. I suppose I shouldn't get too angry with her for being as nosy as I am.

She turned them back around once I came in the room and smiled at me.

"What can I do for you, Eleanore?" It was difficult for me to be civil. I hoped she had come to tell me that she was going to print a retraction about Sylvia.

"Oh, you know, I wanted to see if Rudy could help Oscar paint the porch on the inn next month."

"In November," I said, deciding to temporarily forget about the retraction.

"Yes."

"Isn't there some rule about not painting when it's cold or something?"

She shrugged her shoulders. It was clear that was not why she was here. Then she pointed to the documents she had been peeking at. "I noticed the Dijon name on those papers."

"Yes."

I popped the lid on my can of Dr Pepper, taking solace in hearing the fizz of the carbonation. Eleanore evoked very unpleasant thoughts in me.

"Is that what you're supposed to be working on? I mean, doesn't Sylvia have some tax or land records she wanted done last August that you still don't have finished?" she asked.

"Excuse me?" My blood pressure had just gone up a noticeable amount. My temples hurt.

Her eyes got really big and darted around the room. She pressed her very red lips together, fingered her necklace, and acted innocent.

"Eleanore . . . I'm not sure how you even know about the land records incident, but it's none of your business what I'm working on and what I'm not. But, for the record, I will say that I was working on the history of New Kassel, right over there," I said, and pointed to the computer in the corner. "These just happen to be on my desk because . . ."

"Because?"

"Because I was going over them earlier in the day. I'm not sure what it is that you want or what you're driving at, Eleanore . . . but while you're here there's something I'd like to talk with you about—"

"There was nothing that I wanted, Torie. I truly wanted to know if you thought Rudy would help Oscar with the porch. Oscar wanted to get a group of guys and have a cookout and paint the porch. Really, Torie. You are so sensitive these days."

With that she stood up and walked out of my office. I took a very long, much needed drink of my cold Dr Pepper. Then I took a deep breath and made myself go to the computer.

I stopped just as my fingers reached the keys. She managed to get out of my office without me saying a word to her about the article she had written. My head hurt worse.

Seven

Six hours later, my phone was ringing at the same time that my doorbell was buzzing. Mother answered the phone as I answered the door.

The mayor of New Kassel, Bill Castlereagh, stood on my front porch.

"Hello, Bill," I said as cheerfully as I could. He looked as angry as my rooster does when he gets caught out in the rain. Bill is bald, short, and has a huge belly. He is one of those middle-aged men who are not overweight anywhere except in the midsection. His stomach could rival a midterm pregnancy.

"Torie, for God's sake! What have you done?"

I stood there with a pair of scissors in my hands, and assumed that he was referring to them. "I'm making a banner for the Octoberfest," I said.

"Torie!" my mother yelled. "It's Colin. He wants to speak to you."

Colin? I couldn't get used to my mother calling Sheriff Brooke by his first name. I couldn't treat him like an outsider if everybody was on a first-name basis with him. Rudy had capitulated about two weeks ago.

"Bill, would you come in? I have a phone call. Just for a

minute," I said. He stood just inside the door with his fingers linked just below his belly, waiting impatiently.

"Hello, Sheriff," I said into the phone. I smiled at Bill.

"Torie, I don't know what to say," Colin said.

"About what?"

"You had better not be responsible for this . . . this atrocity or I swear, I will kill you with my own bare hands."

"Jeez, all I'm doing is making one little ole banner."

"Really, Torie, you've gone too far," Bill said to me, unable to keep quiet any longer. "I'm going to have the sheriff arrest you."

"Torie, you have gone too far," the sheriff said.

"Okay, would somebody please shut the heck up and tell me what it is that they think I have done?" I yelled.

Bill shut up with a quick flap of his lower jaw, and surprisingly the sheriff did as well. Finally, after a few seconds of blissful silence, Sheriff Brooke began again in a calm voice.

"Somebody dug up Marie Dijon's grave, and it had better not have been you."

"What?" I felt sick. I felt sick because the thought of somebody digging up that poor woman's grave gave me the creeps. I also felt sick because the sheriff thought I had done it. "Do you really think that I could do something like that?"

"Well, no, not really," Sheriff Brooke said into the phone.

"Then why are you treating me like I did? What made you think such a horrible thing?" I asked.

Both men simultaneously answered, "Eleanore Murdoch."

"Oh, Jesus, Mary, and Joseph!" I stomped my feet a few times and took a deep breath.

"I bet you can tell me why her grave was dug up," the sheriff said.

"Why would somebody dig up her grave?" Bill asked. He was beginning to panic.

"Bill! Take a pill," I said. "Why would either one of you think that I would be able to tell you something about a person digging up Marie's body?"

"Because," the sheriff began, "I think the night you were in her house, you found something that you didn't tell me about. Remember how you told me to listen with an open mind? You gave me your nice little well-thought-out, hokey bunch of bullshit!" he yelled. I pulled the phone away from my ear.

"You don't have to yell at me," I said. "Where are you?"

"I'm standing in the middle of the godforsaken rectory, for Christ's sake—oh, excuse me, Father—and I'm thinking to myself: This smells like Torie O'Shea."

"I'll be there in five minutes."

"No! Don't you dare come down—"

I hung up on him. "Bill, you can either drive yourself or you can ride with me," I said to him. He decided to drive.

•

I pulled my station wagon in behind the mayor's car at the Santa Lucia Cemetery on Jefferson Street and New Bavaria Boulevard. It was dark by now, about eight-thirty in the evening. The mayor didn't want to ride in my car, which was fine with me, because I talked to myself the whole way there and he wouldn't have appreciated anything that I had to say.

The mayor's property backs up to mine, and I have every animal known to mankind living back there. Chickens, rabbits, cats, fifteen species of birds, squirrels. Therefore, he hates me. He's tried to create a city ordinance to get rid of my chickens, but so far he hasn't succeeded. He fancies himself King of New

Kassel, not just mayor. When election times roll around his slogan is "Bill *Kassel*reagh for Mayor of New Kassel." It didn't help our relationship too much when Eleanore Murdoch had a poll one week as to who was New Kassel's most recognized face and I won.

I jumped out of my car almost before it stopped. Sheriff Brooke was standing next to his Festiva with his hands on his hips, looking menacing as hell. Deputy Duran was there as well, including several other CSU personnel.

"If you touch one thing, these men have orders to arrest you on the spot."

"Nice to see you, too, Sheriff. So, you gonna get up to Marie's house and start looking at this like it was a homicide now?" I asked.

"That's none of your business."

I walked over to where Marie's grave was just as the clouds broke into a downpour. I was careful not to step where the yellow police tape was that revealed where the evidence was. The dirt was in a pile off to the right. Her casket was open, her body all humped at one end of the casket, as if the perpetrator had moved her body, searching for something.

"Oh, my God," I said.

"It's not pretty, is it?" Sheriff Brooke said from behind me.

"No," I said. The rain dripped off of my nose. I didn't wipe at it.

"Get a tarp over here," Sheriff Brooke yelled out to the CSU. "The evidence is getting soaked, you morons."

"What did Eleanore Murdoch say about me?"

"She and Bill were both in the library, as was I, when Duran came in and said that somebody had dug up Marie's grave. Your Aunt Bethany asked who could have done such a thing and

Eleanore said you seemed obsessed with Marie and that she had reason to believe—"

"So you just believed her? You didn't give me the benefit of the doubt?"

"If I had stopped and thought about it, I would have realized that it was just Eleanore being vicious. But after you going in Marie's house the other night, well, I just jumped the gun."

"As did the mayor," I added.

Sheriff Brooke nodded.

I noticed where the footsteps of the perpetrator were. The person had dug from the foot of the grave, toes pointed toward the place where the headstone would eventually go. I stood there and tried to mimic what their actions would have been.

"What the heck are you doing?" Sheriff Brooke said.

"Digging a grave." In went my imaginary shovel, feet in the same position.

"Well, when you're finished, get home. You've got no business being out here," he said. "Duran, get over to the Dijon house and get it taped. I don't want anybody in there," he yelled over the roar of the rain.

Duran nodded, got in his patrol car, and took off.

"I think you should check the guest list at her funeral," I said.

"What?"

"There were six or seven people there that were not New Kasselonians. I think those are your suspects. It was one of those people."

"Does Rudy hate it when you act like you know everything?" Sheriff Brooke asked me.

"Despises it. Look, anybody that lives around here for any length of time would know better than to dig up a grave at

Santa Lucia at . . . what time was it exactly that this occurred?"

"About seven forty-five. Father Bingham interrupted him."

"Exactly. Seven forty-five on a Wednesday evening. Father Bingham is playing bingo at the bowling alley, which always lets out at seven-thirty. After he cashes in his chips—he always wins something—and after he blesses everybody, he pulls into the rectory at seven forty-five. Everybody knows that," I said.

That shut him up. It was a wonderful sight to behold. So, while I was at it, I thought I'd just go for the jugular and get it over with.

"Also, he was left-handed."

"How . . ."

"From where his feet were positioned, and where the pile of dirt fell, he had to be shoveling left-handed."

He said nothing, so I thought I'd demonstrate.

"See, the shovel goes in at this angle, when you come up with the dirt, where's the easiest place to pile it? Kinda over your shoulder. If you're digging left-handed, that would be to your right. See?"

He smiled at me. "I don't know how Rudy stays sane."

"I suppose he's just a much bigger man than you," I said, and I walked away, totally drenched. I began veering off toward the rectory instead of my car. I should have known that Sheriff Brooke would notice.

"Hey, Torie. Car's that way."

"I know. I want to see how Father Bingham is."

I was wondering if God finds out about the lies that you tell on sacred ground faster than he finds out about the normal lies?

The church was a white sandstone with arched windows all down the side plus one on each side of the wooden door. They were stained glass, as was the one round window directly above the door. I walked around the church and up the steps of the rectory, opened the door, and walked in. A photograph of the Archbishop of St. Louis smiled down at me. I noticed that the rectory smelled like Rachel's classroom. I'm not real sure what that odor is, and it isn't necessarily an unpleasant odor. It's just a classroomy smell. It's distinct.

"Father Bingham?"

"In here."

He was in his office. I walked in and he sat behind his desk with his head bent over, studying something. He was about sixty, with splotchy skin and sky-blue eyes. His white hair was thin, and he parted it in the middle, of all things. The office was painted in pale blue and it was sparsely decorated with a few biblical paintings and a crucifix.

"Torie, hello," he said. He arose and motioned toward a chair. "Sit down, sit down."

"Oh, no. I'm soaking wet. I just wanted to see how you were. I suppose it was quite a shock coming home to find a grave robber."

"I am just sick over this. Just sick. How's Rudy?"

"Fine."

"And your girls?"

"Fine."

"Haven't seen Rudy in church, since . . . 1986."

"Yes, it was for our wedding."

He only smiled.

"Look, Father. I don't want to take too much of your time. See, I have this problem. A nice gentleman let me borrow his . . . umbrella the other day, and I need to return it to him."

"Yes?"

"It was at Marie Dijon's funeral, and I'm afraid I don't remember his name. Do you think that I could have a look at the guest registry?"

"Well, normally the family gets the registry, but there wasn't anybody to give it to. I think Sister Mary Lucy kept it. She and Marie were good friends. She is quite shook up over this . . . atrocity. Let me ask her."

He picked up the phone, dialed the nunnery, spoke a few seconds, and hung up. "Yes, she has it, I'll be right back," he said.

According to Marie's family charts she had two sisters. I assumed that they were dead, otherwise they would have been at the funeral and there would have been somebody to take the registry.

Father Bingham was gone maybe five minutes, during which time I took a peek to see who had been paying their tithes like they were supposed to. He came in the back door and handed me the registry, a cream-colored book.

"Do you have a pen and paper?" I asked.

He handed me a pen along with a pad of paper and clasped his hands behind his back as I skimmed the pages for names I did not recognize. Andrew Wheaton, Paul Garland . . .

"So, where's the umbrella?" Father Bingham said.

"What?"

"Well, you could sure use it now, couldn't you?"

"Uh, forgot it."

Sally Reuben, Ransford Dooley . . .

"I don't remember it raining the day Marie was buried," he declared.

"No? Hmph."

Of all the things, I had to pick an umbrella.

Lanny Lockhart . . .

Just then I heard the bell buzz and I knew it was Sheriff Brooke. I shoved the piece of paper in my bra, as it was the driest place I could find, and handed the book back to him.

"Well, thanks. I've got to go."

I opened the door to a soaked Sheriff Brooke, smiled at him, and passed on by to my car.

Eight

I decided to drive by the cemetery once before going home to give the whole scene a look from the car. Sometimes you see something from far away that you don't see up close. I had intended to drive by at a crawling speed when I noticed there was somebody behind me. So, I pulled over to let him by, only he pulled over behind me as well. That was odd.

When I pulled away from the curb, so did he. I use the term *he* loosely. In fact, I had no idea if it was a man, woman, or kangaroo driving. It was too dark and the rain only made things worse.

I didn't want to drive home, because then he would know where I lived, providing of course that he didn't already know. I was probably jumping to conclusions anyway, so I thought I'd just drive around town to see if he followed me.

It was at this point that I considered investing in a car phone or one of those cellular thingamajigs. I don't even own a cordless phone. It's times like these that I really feel as though I live during prehistoric times.

I made a quick right on Jefferson and then a quick left onto New Kassel Outer Road, which the car behind me did also. My skin began to tingle. Somebody had just dug up Marie Dijon's grave and now there was a car following me. I was scared. New Kassel Outer Road is just a two-lane blacktop without any streetlights except at junctions or where somebody's driveway was.

I decided to drive to Wisteria and pull into the sheriff's station. Whoever was following me would not follow me into the sheriff's office. Of course, that meant that if I got out of this unscathed, I was going to be in big trouble. Sheriff Brooke would probably arrest me, again. My mother would probably try to ground me for the first time in fifteen years.

God, what a humiliating thought.

In a few minutes I'd be passing my Aunt Emily's farm. I wanted to stop, but knew I couldn't. What if he had a gun and he'd kill us both? No, I had to keep driving. It was amazing to me how the familiar things I saw on this road every day now seemed to take me by surprise and look alien. I never seemed to notice that the log fence on my left was as run-down or as close to the road as it now appeared. I checked the rearview mirror. So far the driver hadn't made any aggressive moves, he just followed with the headlights on low beam.

I turned on the radio and flipped the stations. I needed some music to calm me down. I continued to turn the dial, trying to find something that fit the mood. Beethoven? Too dark for a lonely, deserted stretch of two-lane country road. Huey Lewis? Too happy. Was this really Adam Ant? Wow, too—I don't know, too *something*. Now some girl kept screaming the word *zombie*. No. Definitely don't want to be reminded of dead things that go bump in the night. What was this? U2? Perfect.

So, I drove along singing the words to "I Still Haven't Found What I'm Looking For," thinking it rather apropos. I had not found what I was looking for. I wasn't even sure what it was that I was looking for.

Suddenly the car behind me flashed its brights. He sped up and came within a millimeter of hitting the back of my car. It was so close that I actually prepared myself for the impact and was shaken when it never occurred.

The driver brought the car parallel with mine, which by the way meant that he was in the oncoming traffic's lane. When I glanced over, I could not see who it was. It was too dark, as there were no streetlights at this spot. The driver looked like a male.

We had just passed my Aunt Emily's farm. Her light had been on in the kitchen, and as usual the moon gleamed off the top of her silo. There was only one more marker on the Outer Road before arriving in Wisteria, and that was the intersection with Highway P, which is another two-lane country road leading down to Progress, Missouri. I had about seven more minutes before reaching the Wisteria city limits.

I sped up, not wanting to give the driver the opportunity to sideswipe me, if that was his intention. The car pulled in behind me again. I couldn't figure out what he wanted. He wasn't hurting me, and yet he obviously wanted something. If he thought I was going to pull over, he must have his brain in a vise because I'm not that stupid. He was riding my bumper so close that I could barely see the headlights.

While he was riding right on my tail, something darted across the road from the woods on my right-hand side, directly in front of my car. It was a dog. I slammed on the brakes, and the car plowed right into the back of me. There was no sound of brakes squealing because the driver hadn't had enough time to touch his brakes. I did, however, hear the cringing sound of metal against metal as the two cars crunched together.

I hit my head hard and was stunned for a minute. Blood came from my forehead. I tried to see in the rearview mirror if the driver behind me was all right. I couldn't see anything. He must be slumped over in the seat, I thought.

I sat there a minute, gripping the steering wheel and shaking from head to toe. Of all the stupid . . . I had just totaled my car because a dog ran in front of it. It was an instant reaction. I'm the idiot that will cross into the oncoming traffic so that I won't kill a turtle. I might kill eight people in the process, but the turtle will live! Well, I'd just done the same thing for a dog.

I turned the engine over, and it started with no trouble.

There was still no movement from the car behind me. I had to go check on whoever it was. They could be dead. I couldn't leave them bleeding to death, no matter what the circumstances were. I just couldn't do it.

I found my flashlight in the glove compartment and the baseball bat that I keep under my front seat. I got out of the car, leaving the radio blaring and the door open. I walked slowly back to the other car, dreading every single second of it. The sleeve of my sweatshirt was soaked from the rain and the blood that I kept wiping from my forehead. My heartbeat seemed to thud in my head instead of my chest and I was feeling slightly dizzy.

I knew I was feeling strange from more than just the bump on my head. I was scared of what I'd find in the car. I was scared that either he would be dead and I'd have to see that or he wouldn't be dead. And that could pose a more life-threatening situation for me. I took a few steady deep breaths as I stood by the rear tires of my car.

The back of my car looked as if it had been hit by a Mack truck. Glass was scattered everywhere, and now that I got a good look at the back tires, I knew I couldn't drive the car anywhere. Not to mention the engine of the other car was in the back of my station wagon.

Good going, Torie. This is by far the stupidest thing I have ever done in my entire life.

When I got to the car, I shivered. There was nobody in the front seat or on the floorboard of the car. I checked the backseat. Same thing.

"Damn, damn, damn."

The passenger door was half open, and I assumed that whoever was driving had jumped out the passenger side and disappeared into the woods.

I walked back to my car. When I looked inside, something was in my front seat. It was the dog that I had almost hit.

The cutest little face looked back at me, beating my seat to death with his wagging tail. It was a dachshund. A wiener dog with short red hair.

"Are you hurt?" I asked in my instant oh-you're-so-precious voice.

I sat down next to him and looked him over. I didn't see any blood, bumps, or bruises. There also wasn't any collar or any tag. He wagged his tail, licked me, and genuinely looked very happy to be in my car with me.

"A wiener dog," I said to him. "No, don't give me that look. No, I can't keep you, so don't even try the big brown eyes tactic. Absolutely not."

He rolled over on his back, paws in the air and panting. Clearly, he wanted his belly rubbed.

"My husband will file for divorce and my mother will go live with her sister and then I'll have to listen to how miserable she is because her sister's nuts. I can't keep you," I said to him.

I rubbed his belly. "Of course, my children will elevate me to sainthood."

I shut the door and the dog jumped in my lap, put his paws on the steering wheel, and prepared to drive. "Sorry, we're not

67

going anywhere," I said to him. "We're going to lock the doors and wait until somebody drives by. It should only be a minute or two," I assured him.

He turned around, evidently smelling the blood on me. His nose went to my forehead and he licked at it slightly. I didn't have the strength to stop him. He whined a little and looked back at the road in front of him.

I managed to lock the door and put my hazard lights on. I waited impatiently for a passerby and did not fight the sensation as the road in front of me turned into a dreamlike mist.

Nine

Roses are red, violets are blue, you wrecked the car and your pretty head, too," Rudy said.

I opened my eyes and found Rudy standing over me with a bouquet of red roses. He smiled. His smile was the kind that was contagious. It took up the majority of his face and his whole body seemed to smile with him.

"Hi," I said. I remembered Deputy Newsome telling me that they were taking me to Wisteria General Hospital. I glanced around the hospital room, painted in that perfectly boring gray that only hospitals seem to use. It was either that or the dull cream. I think I actually preferred the gray.

Okay, yes, I was still in Wisteria General. Fairies had not come and taken me home in the middle of the night like I wished they had.

"I told the doctors that the reason you weren't dead was because you were too hardheaded," Rudy said.

"That's the oldest line in the book," I answered.

"But in your case, it's the truth. So are you in any pain?"

"I have a headache," I answered. "It's nothing serious. Just a bump on the head. I was only out for a few minutes."

"I was here last night, do you remember?" he asked.

Vaguely, I remembered him being here. "Yes," I answered.

"We have a problem," Rudy said.

"What's that?"

He put the roses in the vase on the windowsill. "Well, there's this dog . . . a wiener dog. He was in the car with you and I'm not sure what to do with him."

"Oh."

Rudy came over and rubbed my face with the back of his hand. "Colin wants to speak to you."

"I bet he does," I answered. "What did you do with the dog?"

"He's at the house for right now."

Rudy walked around the room, and I got the distinct feeling that there was something that he wanted to tell me. Or ask me. He wore jeans and his T-shirt with the Coca-Cola polar bear on it that the girls got him for Father's Day this year. After ten years of marriage I still say he's got the sexiest butt in a pair of beat-up jeans I've ever seen.

"Look, Colin's outside and he wants to see you. Now," he said. "I told him it depended on how you were feeling."

"I'm fine. Send him in."

Rudy came over and kissed me on the forehead. "You two need to call a truce. I think your mother is really falling for him, Torie. Besides, I know you. Something that starts small eats at you, until you've got a full-blown festered sore."

"He arrested me," I said, indignant.

"I know. And even though I don't agree with him on that, it's something you've just got to get out of your system. He sees you as a woman who thinks she is above the law because most of the time, people here don't make you go by any rules. He decided he'd show you that you do have to answer to the system," Rudy said.

"Yeah, but . . ."

"Don't but me, Torie. He picked the wrong time to do it, I agree. But it was still a lesson that you needed."

I started to tell him that he was just agreeing with Sheriff Brooke because he was a man and this was a man thing. Rudy was just picking on me. But then, the more I thought about it, the more that I knew he was right.

"All right. Send him in," I said.

Rudy left and Sheriff Brooke came in and stood where Rudy had stood before. He was in his full dress uniform, hat and all. It felt as though this was official business. He took his hat off and held it in his right hand.

"Torie," he said as he nodded his head. "How ya feeling?"

"I have a headache," I said and meant it in more ways than one.

"You gonna tell me what happened last night?"

I told him the whole story. "Don't roll your eyes at me, I'm telling the truth. I got my baseball bat and went to see if the person was all right and there was nobody in the car."

"It was a stolen car, which you probably assumed."

"Well, I hadn't given it much thought. It hurts to think too much," I said.

"Did you get a look at the driver?"

"Not really. I'd say it was a man only because he had short hair and was kind of tall."

"Did you get the same list of suspects that I did from the funeral registry?" he asked me.

"Probably," I said.

"And you probably already know that three of them are staying at the Murdoch Inn."

"No, but I was going there today to check it out," I admitted.

He glanced out my window. All I could see from my bed was

the top of the doctors' building next door. It was a sunny day, I could tell that much. The sheriff turned around, pulled his britches legs up at the hips, and leaned against the heat register.

"I propose that we go into business with each other," he said.

"Well, I'm flattered. But I'm not that good with antiques. I mean, I know what they are when I see them, but I can't begin to tell you what they're worth."

"No, not the antiques store," he said to me.

"What do you mean?" I asked.

"I'm going to stop telling you to stop snooping around, as long as you don't do anything illegal. Don't break into anybody's house, that sort of thing. Don't endanger yourself. If you can do whatever it is that you do without breaking the law, have at it."

"What's the catch?"

"Nothing. If it doesn't endanger you to snoop around and ask questions, then I'm not going to tell you not to anymore."

"I get it. You think that if you tell me it's okay that it will take all the fun out of it and I'll just stop on my own. It won't work, because that's not why I do it. All I know is that I get something in my head and it won't leave until I have an answer for it that is satisfactory. It drives me nuts. That's it. Curiosity. There are no hidden motives," I said.

"Whatever you say. All I know is sometimes I need the input of outsiders. It helps to get a fresh approach."

"Oh, paleeze," I said. "I'm choking from all the cow manure in here."

"I'm serious. You helped me a lot on the Zumwalt case. And you made the right call on this one. Duran missed the two glasses on the table bigger than day. So if you want to give me advice in the future I'll accept it," he said. "As long as you don't break any laws or any bones, get yourself killed, or get anybody else killed. And of course you have to tell me everything you find. But don't tell anybody else," he said.

"I can't tell anybody? It's no fun if I can't brag about it."

"You brag, the deal's off."

"Oh, all right," I agreed.

He stood up and pulled a clear plastic bag out of his pants pocket. "Is this yours?" he asked.

It was an inhaler for asthma.

"No. Why would you think that?"

"I found it in Marie's house. Marie did not have asthma."

"Where in the house did you find it?" I asked.

"In the entrance from the living room to the kitchen," he said.

"That's what I tripped over," I said more to myself than to him.

"What?"

"Well, I stepped on something in the house that was sort of round and I fell. It was in the same area."

"I'm betting whoever was there that night dropped it."

"Yeah, and I'll bet that if he or she didn't have an extra, then they are having to get a refill."

"I'm already checking the surrounding pharmacies. I'll get a list of everybody that got a refill or a replacement in the last week."

He was silent now. Neither one of us had much more to say to each other.

"Anything you want to tell me?" he asked.

I thought about the photocopies that Camille had. "Not yet. Maybe by this evening I will have something," I said. "Maybe something from Marie's."

He raised his eyebrows.

I didn't think there was any point in getting Camille in-volved in all of this if there was no reason to. I would just wait and see what the documents said first. Then I'd tell him.

"Okay," he said as he put his hat back on. "I hope your headache goes away soon," he said.

"Oh, I doubt that it will."

Ten

I was released from Wisteria General at noon. Rudy came with Mary to drive me home. Mom was waiting at the door as I came up the steps.

"I can make you a bed on the couch if you want. I don't think you should be climbing too many steps," she said.

"I'm fine. Really. I'm just a little stiff. All I did was bump my head. They just kept me overnight for observation."

She looked tired, I noticed. Dark smudges lay underneath her eyes, ruining her otherwise perfect creamy complexion. I wondered if she was tired from just being up in the middle of the night worrying about me, or from being up all night convincing Sheriff Brooke to call his truce. I was certain that Mother had pep-talked him just as Rudy had with me. This whole idea was probably Rudy and Mother's to begin with.

"Is that Speed Racer I hear coming in the door?" My grandmother of eighty-one years came in from the kitchen.

"Hello, Granny," I said.

She gave me a hug. It was a warm, nurturing, loving hug. Then she smacked me on the butt as hard as she could. "You need a good spankin', that's what you need. You better take that offensive driving course that Tobias was telling us about at bingo last week."

"Granny," I pleaded as I rubbed my backside.

"I mean it," she said. Her eyes were like my mother's, dark-brown and large. Her skin was creamy and clear, too. But Granny had a square face and much higher, more prominent cheekbones than my mother.

"I'll be fine," I said.

"Well, I'm making you chicken and dumplings," she said.

That settled it. I wouldn't feel bad for long. Chicken and dumplings was a cure-all. At least for me.

"And," my mother added, "I made a lemon chiffon pie."

Heck, I'd be doing a hoedown by sunset.

I went up to my bedroom intending to lie down to take a nap. But I ended up in the office instead. I pulled some books off of the shelf and started thumbing through them. I wasn't really looking for anything in particular, just everything in general. I was looking for information that would tell me the state of France in 1756. *The Age of Voltaire* seemed like a good place to start.

The phone rang.

"Hello?" I answered.

"Hello, Victory."

"Oh, Sylvia. I probably won't be in today, but I will be in tomorrow. I know the Octoberfest starts in three days."

"That's quite all right, Victory. I'd like for you or Rudy to come by the Gaheimer House sometime today. I have something for you."

"Oh." There was not much else I could say to that. Sylvia was not the type of person to give or buy things for people. I don't think I'd ever received a gift from Sylvia in my life.

"I'm in no hurry. Did you find enough bands for the blue-grass festival?" Sylvia asked.

"Yes. It'll work out great. There are thirty days to the Octoberfest, so I found ten bands. Each one will play three days."

"Wonderful. You can fill me in on the rest tomorrow," she said and hung up.

Wonderful? Nothing was ever *wonderful* with Sylvia. I glanced at my watch. It was two o'clock. I suddenly remembered that I had to pick up the translations from Camille at three. I put the book on my desk and headed downstairs.

"Rudy, can I borrow your van?" I asked.

"What?"

"I have an appointment that I forgot all about at three o'clock."

My mother looked at me as if I had grown fangs and my grandmother looked as though she was going to smack my other cheek.

"I'll be back before Rachel is home from school. It will be in plenty of time to eat dinner."

Silence.

"I really cannot miss this appointment."

"I'll drive you, how's that?" Rudy asked.

"Okay, fine. But I have to stop by the Gaheimer House on the way out," I said as I grabbed my purse. "And I have to stop by Wilbert Reaves's office."

"Torie!" my mother said.

"What?" I asked when I reached the door. She didn't say anything for a moment.

"Never mind."

I shut the door and went down the steps. I climbed into

Rudy's silver Transport and buckled my seatbelt. "I really appreciate this, Rudy."

"Mmm-huh."

"Really. Did you feed the chickens this morning? Hey, where was the dog?"

"Fritz was in the backyard."

"Fritz?" I asked. I stared at him in disbelief. "What? You named the dog? It's not our dog. How could you name the dog? How could you name him Fritz? I found him. Don't I have any say-so in what his name is?"

"He looks like a Fritz. I couldn't help it," he said. He put his blinker on and turned. "Rachel and Mary went spastic when they saw the dog."

"Yeah. I'll bet my mother did, too."

"Well, I wasn't too thrilled, I'll have you know. But how was I supposed to tell them they couldn't keep the dog when he was licking their faces and wagging his tail? And every time Mary took a step, she'd trip over him because he was right under her feet. You should've seen it, Torie. It was so funny."

"It's not our dog."

I was beginning to wonder if it wasn't Rudy's head that had gotten hit instead of mine.

"I know that. I put an ad in the paper and I told the girls if nobody answered it in a week that they could keep it."

"Rudy! My mother—"

"I couldn't help it," he said. "You should've never put the dog in your car in the first place."

"Well, I didn't. He sort of found me."

Rudy pulled into Wilbert Reaves's parking lot and turned off the van. We walked in and smiled at Jamie Thorley seated behind the desk. The building always reminds me of one of those cheap mobile homes on the inside. Not the really nice deluxe ones, but the tacky ones with the plain brown paneling and indoor/outdoor carpet.

"Hello, Rudy," she said. She has the biggest, bluest eyes on the planet and her brain is pretty much as clear as her eyes. She smiled as big as she could, reminding me of those child stars on Broadway.

I was forgotten for the moment. My husband is as cute as a bug's ear and all the young girls think so, too.

"Hello, Jamie," he answered her. "Torie needs to see Wilbert."

"Oh, hiya, Torie. He's got a client in there right now," she said.

Just then, Wilbert walked out of his office with a very pretty woman in her mid-fifties. Wilbert is about thirty-eight and short. He would make a good horse jockey if he lost about twenty pounds.

"Torie," he said. "I was just thinking about you. Seems we had a little mixup the other night."

"Yes, Jamie said you'd be at Marie's around seven. You never showed up."

"I said I'd be at Pierre's around seven."

I looked at Jamie who was chewing her gum to death. "Hey, Dijon, Pierre. They were both French. Coulda happened to anybody."

"Of course it could have," Wilbert cooed. "Hey, Rudy. How's your golf game coming?" he asked when he suddenly realized that Rudy was in the room.

"I don't play golf," Rudy answered.

"Of course you don't," Wilbert said.

"Have you got a few minutes?" I asked him.

"Not really. Oh, hey, this is Marie's sister. Yvonne Meza-laine."

"Hello," she said in a French accent.

"Sister?" My mind was racing. Marie's family tree mentioned two sisters and neither one of them was named Yvonne.

"Half sister, really," she said. "And you are?"

Her family tree did not mention any half sister at all.

"A friend of hers. A dear, dear friend," I lied. Rudy was giving me a weird look. I just smiled at him. "She never mentioned you, Ms. Mezalaine. As a matter of fact, you're not on her family charts either."

"She never put me on her charts. We had a row many years ago. So, you've seen the charts then?"

"Oh, yes, in detail. Studied them in fact."

Her green eyes narrowed on me. I caught a glimpse of Rudy doing the same thing.

"I'm sorry, Ms. Mezalaine," Wilbert interjected. "This is Victory O'Shea. She is our resident historian and, you know, historical person."

"Aah," she said. "Your name is Irish. But you have some French, no? You look it."

"Yes. My paternal grandmother was all French. My husband is the Irishman."

"Aah," she said again. "It is an impressive family tree, is it not?"

"Mine?"

"No, Marie's."

"And yours, too," I corrected her.

She looked at me for a minute, confused.

"You said Marie's, but it would be yours, too, at least part of it. And we're related, actually, too."

Rudy coughed and tried to walk nonchalantly to the door. That's marriage talk for *let's get the heck out of here, now.*

"How so?" Yvonne said.

"We're both descendants of Charlemagne."

She only smiled then and turned back to Wilbert. "I go now, Monsieur Reaves. We will speak again."

"Yes, of course," he said and watched as the elegant woman slinked out of his office and left me in complete silence.

"Can't talk now, Torie. Catch me later," he said as he shut himself behind the doors to his office. I really didn't care for Wilbert Reaves too much, and it was things like this that just affirmed my dislike all the more.

•

"I'll wait here," Rudy said as he pulled in front of Camille Lombarde's house.

"Why?" I asked.

"Because then you'll feel guilty for leaving me out here with the car running and you won't stay as long," he said.

"That's what you think," I answered him.

He gave me a condescending look and turned off the engine.

"I'll hurry," I said.

We had arrived maybe fifteen minutes early. I didn't think Camille would mind. She looked tired when she answered the door. It appeared as if she got out of bed, took a shower, and then didn't do any of her normal grooming, like curling her hair or applying makeup.

"Is it time already?" she asked.

"I'm a few minutes early," I said as I stepped into her foyer.

Some of the photocopies lay out on the table in the den, the others I could not see. She offered me a seat, which I took.

"Well, I don't have them all done," she announced.

"What do you mean?"

"I couldn't get them all finished. The ones that I didn't finish are in my safe. You can take these with you and come back for the others, when I get them translated."

"Oh" was all I managed.

"They're quite interesting. I translated one of the coded ones, and tried to decipher the code all night. I had no luck. I suppose I shouldn't have done that; then I might have gotten them all finished."

She handed me a piece of paper that was in her handwriting.

"Go ahead, read it. That's the letter to your countess."

I read silently.

April 1756

Dearest Countess,

It has been many years since we've seen each other. I am eighty-two now, and have been diagnosed with liver ailment. I shall not live out the year. It is my wish that you accept my confession bravely.

The rumor of Louis XIV having a twin brother at birth is but that . . . a rumor. I know this for certain. In 1694 I was called to the island of Sainte Marguerite. His Majesty wished to make a point by giving me the body of your beloved cousin, the former Archbishop of Reims. It is a fact that he died in 1694 and that he was replaced by his valet from 1694 until the valet's death in 1703, at the Bastille. At the time Louis did not know of my connections to your family, or he would have never entrusted me with the disposal of your cousin's body. And it has taken me this long to confess it, out of sentimental duty and the fact that your family was right. You and I know, only too well, the terrible betrayal in the Order from 1700 to 1730. They were no longer a threat to His Majesty in 1703. If I had acted in 1694, when I knew the truth, that might have given you time.

*Events are in motion to rectify the damage done by the inter-
nal war. Fear not! You and yours will be avenged!*

*Your cousin is buried at the Château Blanchefort near Rennes.
His information to use against the crown is entact, and some-
where safe. Had I but known then that your family was right . . .
I would have done differently. Please forgive me.*

*It is up to you, dearest Countess, to see to it your cousin's
heirs receive their due. You must not fail.*

Respectfully Yours,
Antoine

Wow. I looked up at Camille, who had been watching me
closely. Her gaze darted around the room and finally landed on
me again.

"I don't want to excite you," she said. "But I think that the
information that this man had against the French crown is in
those other photocopies that I have in my safe."

"Wow."

"Here's another letter that I translated. If I'm not mistaken,
it was written here in the United States to somebody back in
France. Read it."

December 1922

Philippe,

*Of which we were speaking earlier: Indeed it is pertaining to
35–40 and 90–95. Just as we had planned. Who is the heir?
Sauniere was a fool. It was but a part, one minuscule part, of
what the Order is capable. This should have been taken care of
long ago. Know that what we speak of is as it should be. Please
send me appropriate documentation and code that you have received and understood this.*

*I grow weary . . . three have died because of this already.
There are many Germans here. I long for France.*

Awaiting,
Gaston

She handed me one last piece of paper that looked like some sort of game. "This is one of the coded documents. It's the only one that I translated."

I stared at it for the longest time as if it would reveal itself to me. Instead, my headache got worse.

16 5 19 18 5 5 11 – 18 24 4 20 19 1 – 25 4 8 5 – 6 11 15 –
25 3 20 19 1 – 12 6 19 – 6 11 15 – 11 4 11 5 19 1 – 25 4 8
5 – 6 11 15 – 11 4 11 5 19 1 – 12 3 11 14 – 19 24 5 20 5

And on it went for another ten or fifteen lines like that. I didn't know what to say. I didn't know what to think, for that matter. Camille looked at me as if she expected me to say something.

"I . . . uh . . . I don't know what to make of this."

"I don't either."

"Well, surely, this information can't do anybody any harm, can it? I mean, there is no crown in France any longer for it to hurt."

"What makes you think somebody would get hurt over it?"

I only shrugged.

"What you've got here is the find of the century," Camille said. "If for no other reason than from a strictly antiquarian viewpoint."

"Well, maybe you shouldn't translate the rest of them. Maybe I should just turn them over to a university, or even the French government."

"You're spooked," Camille said. "Is there something you're not telling me?"

"No. I just don't care what they say anymore. This is too weird," I said.

"Oh, you can't tempt me like this. You have to give me one more night. I have to know what they say now. My curiosity is piqued."

Nobody knew that she had them. What would one more day hurt? I really felt uneasy about leaving the photocopies. But I couldn't make a big deal out of it or it would only make her suspicious, and I truly didn't know what I had. I knew I had something big. And I was half convinced that this is what the grave robber was looking for.

"Oh, I suppose," I said. "But I will be here at three tomorrow to get them whether you have them finished or not."

She smiled triumphantly and clapped her hands. "Oh, good," she said. "I have not been so excited about a project in many years." She clasped her hands together.

"Well, I really have to get going," I said. "My husband is waiting out in the car."

"Oh," she said. "So he is being antisocial."

"No, he thinks if he stays out in the car, I won't take so long."

She looked at me, confused.

"Well, I have a tendency to talk and talk and genuinely take too long at whatever it is I'm doing. My grandmother has fixed me dinner and he doesn't want us to be late," I said.

"Oh, how lovely," she said. "What happened to your head?" She pointed to my small white bandage on my forehead.

"Oh, a fender bender last night and I hit my head. I'm all right," I said.

"Oh, good," she said. "Oh, I just remembered. I made a red velvet cake, and I know how much you like it. Let me get you some to take with you."

She left the room and I was alone in her den. It was the first time I'd ever been alone in the room and had a chance to look at anything in detail. There was a small painting of Jesus on the cross, looking up into the heavens. The painting was located next to the window, in one of the few places with any wall space left in the den.

There were tons of books on the shelves that went from floor to ceiling, even at the top. Old photographs in pewter frames sat on a few of the shelves. There was a beautiful crucifix that was done in cherry wood with Christ carved out of ivory. Her worktable was long and had huge clawed feet. These details made the room awe-inspiring.

Camille came back in the room with her usual grace. "Here you go," she said and handed me the cake, wrapped and ready to go. "I'll see you tomorrow at three," she said, pleased.

"Yes. Tomorrow at three."

I walked outside to find Rudy snoozing with the radio blaring. It was some talk show. Somebody's ex-mother-in-law married their father and they were trying to figure out the relationship. It would have bored me to sleep, too.

"Rudy," I said. "Wake up."

"Hmm? I'm awake."

Why do men always do that?

We pulled away from the curb as a chill ran down my arms. I could not figure out why somebody would dig up a grave looking for documents that could not have any bearing on political situations of today. There was always the possibility that the documents themselves were worth lots of money. But it was obvious that all the documents were not written by the same author or even in the same century. I was totally and thoroughly perplexed.

Eleven

I'm sorry, Sylvia," I said as I entered the Gaheimer House the next morning. "Rudy and I ran out of time yesterday."

"Don't worry about it," she answered.

Wilma came out of the kitchen with a cup of hot chocolate for me. She locked eyes with me and I knew something was wrong. Her usually cheerful disposition was subdued.

Sylvia went to the phone table in the hall next to the soda machine and picked up a small black leather book. She handed it to me and turned away. She gave no explanation as to what it was or what I was supposed to do with it.

I looked to Wilma and she shook her head.

"Sylvia," I began. "What is this?"

"It's Hermann's diary. I want you to have it."

Now I understood what was bothering Wilma. It was completely unlike Sylvia to let anything out of her sight that belonged to Hermann Gaheimer. Why would she suddenly hand this over to me?

"Why?"

"Oh, for once, Victory, don't overanalyze everything, just take the book."

"I don't want it. You give it to somebody else," I said. Sylvia would never give it to anybody else. She had spent sixty-odd years building a veritable shrine in the memory of Hermann Gaheimer and the only person besides herself that she trusted anything with was me. I knew she would not give it to anybody else.

"I've never even read it," she announced.

"Then why do you want me to have it?" I asked.

"Because I can't throw it away, but I don't want to read it either. I'm afraid of what it might say."

In other words she was afraid that Hermann may have blamed her for the death of Sophie as much as she had all of these years. And if he had blamed her in some way, it would destroy Sylvia's carefully crafted fantasy.

I considered being stubborn and refusing to take the diary anyway. But Sylvia had just admitted to being afraid of something, and I couldn't remember that ever happening. Wilma stood there twisting her handkerchief into knots. She was clearly concerned over my next sentence.

"All right. Fine. I accept your gift, Sylvia. Thank you very much," I said.

"How's your mother?" Wilma asked me. She was obviously anxious to change the subject.

"She's fine, Wilma. Just fine." Sylvia stood with her back to me looking out of the kitchen window. I had no idea if she was actually looking at anything or not. I imagined that what she saw at that moment was the New Kassel of days gone by.

"Thank you, Wilma, for the hot chocolate. I have to get over to the Murdoch Inn." I handed her the mug back and left quietly.

•

It would be a trick to get in the Murdoch Inn and speak to the three suspects that were staying there without confronting

Eleanore. I was saving that mess for a later date. I did not want to deal with Eleanore now.

I sat in the north hallway at the top step and hoped that Eleanore would not walk by. I did hope, however, that one of the people that I saw at Marie's funeral would. I know what you're thinking. I could be here all day. Well, I was prepared for that and had brought *The Name of the Rose* along for company.

Two hours later I realized that I was paying entirely too much attention to the book I was reading instead of who was walking by. I put the book down, rubbed the back of my neck, and yawned. I leaned all the way backward to let the kinks out of my back and saw a man walking toward me. Of course he was upside down to me, so I wasn't sure who it was.

"Locked out of your room?" he asked cheerfully as he walked by.

He was definitely one of the people at Marie's funeral.

"Oh, excuse me," I said. I stood up and held out my right hand, minus the book. "I'm Torie O'Shea," I said. "I'm the historian here in town, and I was wondering if I could have a word with you?"

"I'm from out of town," he said as he shook my hand. He was about six feet, but weighed nearly three hundred pounds. He had a thick beard with a generous amount of white in it. His mustache was much darker, with virtually no gray or white at all. The hair on his head was thin. It didn't seem fair that his face would sport so much hair and his head would not. He wore suspenders over his white shirt to hold up his dark slacks, which only pronounced his thick middle all the more.

"Yes, I know. It's about Marie Dijon," I said.

His eyes were small, so small that I wasn't even sure what color they were and I was looking right at them. "What do you want?" he said, losing his friendly manner.

"Let's go somewhere and talk. I don't want to stand in the hallway."

"All right. But make it snappy. I have an appointment in an hour," he said.

"I'm sorry," I said as we went down the steps. "I've gotten your name confused with one of the other guests. What was your name again?"

"Lanny. Lanny Lockheart," he said.

I took him out the side entrance because I didn't want to run the risk of being seen by Eleanore. We walked across the grounds and headed for the wharf. We were in plain view of any number of buildings and people so I wasn't worried about my safety. I basically wanted to make sure that nobody was close enough to hear what we discussed.

"Marie gave me her family charts," I said to him.

"Yes?"

"Along with pages and pages of documentation."

"What sort of documentation?" he asked.

"Birth certificates, histories written by scholars on her family, that sort of thing. You know she had quite an impressive pedigree. She was the closest thing to royalty I think this town has ever had."

"I'm afraid I can't help you with any of that. I am a professor at Loyola, but this is not my cup of tea," he said.

"A professor of what?"

"I have my doctorate in theology and history."

"Really? Well, how did you know Marie?" I asked.

"She was a student of mine. I hadn't been a teacher for very long. I was barely eight years older than her. We had a wonderful friendship," he said.

"Oh, I'm so glad that you got to see her before she died."

"I did not," he said. "I never got the chance to. I came into town and we were supposed to meet the next day, but she never showed."

"Did you call the police or anything? I mean, she was expecting you, wasn't she? I would hardly think that she would stand up a lifelong acquaintance coming all the way from Chicago," I said.

"Yes, I did. They told me she had to be missing for a certain amount of time before they would do anything. They also said that she often left town without telling people."

That much was true. Marie did take long trips, short trips, trips of all kinds. She was always packing her car with her luggage. I could see why the sheriff's department would think that.

"Where were you Tuesday night and Wednesday morning?" I asked.

"I was with a colleague of mine. Andrew Wheaton."

"Oh," I said.

"Am I being investigated?" he asked. "Because it feels like it." He was starting to get angry.

"No. I didn't mean to give that impression. I was just curious. You know, the sheriff thinks she may have been murdered."

Mr. Lockheart looked over his shoulder toward the inn very nervously. "What do you mean?"

"Somebody ransacked her grave," I said. "They are beginning to suspect foul play. I just thought maybe you might have an idea of why somebody would want to kill her." I had no idea if he was buying anything that I said. But he was definitely restless all of a sudden.

"My God," he said. "How horrible."

I wasn't sure if his words stemmed from fear or loathing. But he was certainly disturbed by the news of grave robbers.

"She's been buried at least a week," I said. "Why are you still in town?" It had just occurred to me that at least three people who were at Marie's funeral and outsiders to New Kassel were still in town and at the Murdoch Inn. Why were they sticking around?

"Not that it's any of your business," he said, "but there is a convention going on at Washington University. Andrew and I decided to stay and attend it."

There were tons of hotels closer to St. Louis than this. But his answer was still believable. "I see," was all I said.

"Look, Ms. O'Shea, I really have to be going. I don't want to miss my appointment. I'm sorry I could not help you," he said and walked back toward the inn. He did not wait for me to say thank you or even farewell. He just left.

He was suddenly a very irritated man.

NEW KASSEL GAZETTE

THE NEWS YOU MIGHT MISS
by Eleanore Murdoch

R udy O'Shea has found a lost wiener dog and wants the owner to come forth. Of course, he stressed the point that if the owner didn't want to come forth, he and his family would be just as happy to keep it. My sources tell me that they've already named it and bought it a doghouse, although they rarely let him out.

Speaking of the O'Sheas, Torie suffered a nasty bump in a recent fender bender. Hope you feel better, Torie.

Elmer Kolbe wants to remind everybody about the new city ordinances this year when we have our big bonfire. You can't burn anything except wood!

Oh, and Father Bingham has put up a reward for any information on that terrible incident that happened in his cemetery. Grave robbers! In New Kassel! The reward is from the sisters' quilting fund. $897.26.

Until next time.

Eleanore

Twelve

M ommy," Mary said.

"What, dear?"

"Can I wear a dress tomorrow?" she asked. She stood at the top of the stairs waiting to come into my office at home. She walked in and over to my desk where I was sitting. She held her hands behind her back and I was fairly certain that she was hiding something back there.

"What'cha got behind your back?" I asked.

She grinned mischievously and produced her new pair of black patent leather dress shoes. She said nothing. She only looked around the room trying to be nonchalant.

"You want to wear a dress tomorrow so that you can wear your new shoes. Is that it?"

She shook her head yes, her round cheeks pink with the blessed health that many of us have in America. Her face had the look of good nutrition, good care, and lots of love.

"Do you think you can ride the rides and have fun in those shoes?" I asked her.

Again she shook her head yes, her green eyes hopeful.

"Okay," I said, "you can wear them."

"Thanks," she said and hugged my neck. The shoes clanked the side of my head in the process, but I didn't mind. She headed toward the steps and sat down at the top to put on her dress shoes. She was in her *Little Mermaid* nightgown, but she didn't care. She wanted to wear her new shoes. She was only four, and already she loved shoes. Especially new ones that were black and shiny.

As she went down the steps, Sheriff Brooke came up. He had on his fishing cap, a black T-shirt that advertised some kind of motor oil, and, of course, blue jeans. His scruffy boots scraped across my hardwood floor as he came into my office.

"Hello," he said.

"Are you off today?" I asked.

"Yes," he said. He walked around my office, stopping every now and then to study something. He fingered a copy of *Under the Lilacs* by Louisa May Alcott. It had been my Grandma Keith's. "I think I'm gonna go fishin'. I thought maybe Rudy would like to go, but Jalena said he's in Minneapolis," he said.

"Yeah. Some plumbing fixture convention," I said. "He should be home late tonight. Maybe he'll go with you tomorrow."

"But tomorrow's the first day of the Octoberfest."

"Oh, I forgot." How could I forget that? I'd been organizing judges for the bake-off, the quilt show, and the Best Pumpkin Recipe contest, not to mention all the bands.

He passed by a painting of a ship. The ship was nearly all black, a silhouette against a mauve sunset. "Your mother paint that?" he asked me.

"Yes, she did."

"I keep telling her she's good," he said.

Then he came to a picture of Christ. It was decoupaged onto

a piece of wood. Jesus was all illuminated in golden hues as he reached out with his right hand as if to bless you. His gown was of rich burgundy and green. The decoupage had started to crack, giving it an ancient appearance.

"My father made that for his mother," I said to Sheriff Brooke. "In 1953. He was thirteen years old."

As he looked around the office, I did, too. Most of the things hanging or sitting out were not necessarily things that I would have bought for myself, but they were given to me. They represented something. I wondered if all people were like me.

"Who's she?" he asked as he pointed to a photo on my desk.

"That is my mother's grandmother. Isn't she beautiful?"

"Yes, she is," he said.

"So, what can I do for you, Sheriff?"

He glanced at my stack of books on the end of my desk.

"*Chronicles of the Crusades, The Hero With a Thousand Faces, A History of Secret Societies.* Gee. A little light reading there?" he said.

"The heavier the better," I said.

"I was just curious," he said. "You never did get back to me. You said that you might have some information for me."

Camille. I had to go and pick up the rest of the translations in about two hours. "Okay, I'll have something for you later today, but I don't know what it is."

"What do you mean?"

"I've got tons of information, but none of it makes any sense."

"How?" he asked.

"I think I have what the grave robber was looking for."

"I knew it!" he yelled. "Torie—"

"Wait," I said. "I've had this all along. I had this before you ever set down the guidelines to our little game."

"Why didn't you tell me at the hospital?" he asked.

"It's documents. In French, no less. I'm having them translated, and I didn't want to drag the translator into the middle of everything if I didn't have to. I'm not sure this is what the grave robber was looking for, although what I found was hidden. Don't look at me like that, I found it quite by accident. Anyway, I just didn't want to involve her."

"You've already involved her. What if somebody followed you to her place?"

The blood drained from my face and I felt cool and clammy all over. I had not thought of that. "Oh, God," I said. I reached for the phone.

"What are you doing?" Sheriff Brooke asked me.

"I'm going to call her," I said, dialing. "Hello? Camille. It's Torie. I've just been informed that there is reason to believe that those documents may be dangerous to whoever has them."

"What on earth are you talking about?" she asked.

"Just lock your doors and don't let anybody in until I get there. I'm coming over right now with the sheriff to get those papers," I said and hung up. I looked up in fear at Sheriff Brooke.

"Let's go," he said.

"I didn't think about anybody following me. What about here at my house?" I asked. "I could get everybody killed."

"Chances are whoever it is is not going to take a chance of coming into a home with five people living in it. One of whom dates the sheriff. You also have a security system. I'm sure you'll be quite safe. You're a very well-known person," he said.

I appreciated the fact that he was trying to make me feel better. And I agreed with him to some extent. But Camille, well, she was a sitting duck. I just seemed to keep topping my peak of stupidity this week.

•

We arrived at Camille's house thirty minutes later. My worst fears came to life as we walked up to the steps of her home and saw that the front door had been wedged open with something. The wood had been knicked severely.

"Get back to the car," he said. We had come in his bright yellow Festiva instead of his patrol car. He picked up his car phone and dialed 911. The St. Louis Police Department would be arriving soon.

"You stay in this car," he said as he pulled his gun out of the glove compartment. It was not his jurisdiction in any way, but if the situation warranted it, I knew Sheriff Brooke would fire his weapon. "I'm going in. We could be losing precious time. If you get out of this car, I will shoot you in the kneecap. Do you hear me?" he asked.

"Yes," I managed to say. I doubted that he would really shoot me, but I wouldn't put some other form of bodily harm past him. I would stay in the car. Besides, I didn't know who was inside Camille's house. I didn't want to come face-to-face with a killer.

He disappeared into the front door and I choked on my heart. What had I done? It seemed like an hour before the police showed up, but in reality it was only four minutes. I had not heard any shots fired. That could either mean that there was no armed assailant in the house, or it could mean that the assailant could kill with his bare hands, and Sheriff Brooke didn't get a chance to shoot him. I could always think of something morbid at just the right moment.

One police officer came over to me. He was a sharp-looking black man, completely confident.

"Sheriff Brooke went in there," I said and pointed. "He's not come out."

"Have you heard anything?" he asked.

"Not a sound."

Just then, Sheriff Brooke came from around the alley. "Back here," he said. "Get an ambulance."

Get an ambulance. The words cut through me. I started to open the door and get out.

"Stay!" he barked as if I were a dog.

"Is she dead?" I cried out. *Please, God, don't let her be dead.* He looked at me as though he wasn't going to answer. "You tell me if she's dead!" I demanded.

I was crying now. Camille was an old acquaintance and if I'd just gotten her killed, I would never be able to sleep ever again.

"No," he said. "She's not dead. She should be," he added. "But she's not."

The relief was incredible. I sat back down in the car and breathed deeply. In through the nose. Out through the mouth. My chin trembled and my self-control threatened to give way. But enough heavy breathing and my muscles stopped jumping and I eventually returned to normal. She wasn't dead. Now I was frantic over what had actually happened to her. All I could think was that I hoped it wasn't painful.

Finally, after ten minutes of pure hell and being stared at by the accumulating crowd, I would finally get some answers. Sheriff Brooke came onto the sidewalk and then over to his car. He got in, returned his gun to the glove compartment, and glared at me.

"She was in the garage."

"What?" I asked.

"The garage in the back. It's separate from the house."

"Yes? And? Don't make me guess. Out with it!"

"She'd been locked inside the garage. Whoever it was started the engine of her car and then locked the doors with the engine running. Camille couldn't get to it to turn it off," he said. "Nor could she get out of the garage. There are two small windows and she broke one, but they are too small for her to climb through."

"My God," I said. "Was she hurt any other way?"

"No. The guy broke in and forced her out to the garage."

"Oh, Lord. Was the car still running when you got to her?" I asked.

"No. It ran out of gas," he said as he ran his fingers through his sandy hair. "The papers are gone."

"What?" I said in disbelief. No denying it now. She was nearly killed because of those documents. That was exactly what the grave robber, who was probably one and the same person, was looking for as well.

"Will she be okay?" I said.

"I'm not a doctor, Torie. But I think she might be okay."

It was my fault. Camille had nearly died because of me. Actually, it was because of Marie. But she would never have been in danger if it weren't for me. I brought this to her doorstep. I tried to tell myself that I had no way of knowing when I brought these photocopies to her that they were what Marie died for. I had no way of knowing that somebody would follow me to Camille's house, I assured myself. So why didn't I feel any better?

Camille would be all right. But I didn't know if I would be.

Thirteen

The Winer Brothers fiddled and picked and fiddled some more of their bluegrass music to a crowd of a few hundred people. It was the first day of the Octoberfest. My grandmother had a front row seat with her name on it, and it would remain her seat throughout the month of October.

Rudy and Sheriff Brooke took the girls to ride the Ferris wheel and the merry-go-round. At seven, Rachel wanted to ride the bigger kids' rides. Mary on the other hand was the daredevil in real life, but wanted no part of rides that went faster than a snail's pace. I think it was a control issue.

I was on the sidewalk of the Gaheimer House, awaiting my crowd of tourists so I could begin the next tour. I was dressed in a period gown of the 1890s. It was one of my favorites to look at but one of the least comfortable. It was not the gown itself that was uncomfortable but the corset I had to wear with it, a "Swanbill" corset made from black coutil. It was effective in reducing full-figured gals to that wonderful perfect hourglass of the 1890s. And it hurt like hell. I couldn't breathe, and had to forget about eating altogether.

The gown was a lavender dinner dress with huge puffy sleeves and a lace-trimmed neckline with a few flowers as well.

I only wish that I could achieve this figure without maiming myself. Sylvia had the gowns designed just for me. I had seven different gowns from all different time periods and I'm sure they cost a blooming fortune. Something else that Sylvia paid for.

"Excuse me, ma'am," a voice said from behind me.

I turned around and expected a tourist who needed help finding a particular shop or event. I was face-to-face with one of the out-of-town mourners at Marie's funeral.

"Andrew Wheaton," he said and extended his hand. He was young, possibly late twenties. He reminded me of an all-American athlete, the kind who dated the homecoming queen. He was about five-feet-ten and was nicely shaped in all the right places. It was the type of physique that one gets from using muscles that one doesn't normally use.

I held out my hand and said, "I'm—"

"Victory O'Shea," he finished. He was lightly freckled with blue eyes and a million-dollar smile. It was bizarre the way he acted as if he knew me very well.

"Yes," I said. "What can I do for you?"

"I thought you were looking for me," he said.

Which I had been. So that was his game. He'd come to me before I had the chance to go to him and then it would appear as though he had nothing to hide.

"I can't figure for the life of me where you would have heard that," I said to him.

"Lanny Lockheart and I spoke yesterday over lunch. He said that you had some disturbing news about Marie," Andrew explained.

"Did he tell you what that news was?"

"Yes."

"Then what do you need to see me for?"

He seemed a little flustered by that question.

"Well, uh, do the police have any suspects?" he asked me as he shifted his feet.

"Yes. All kinds," I said.

"Well, I've not been questioned," he stated.

"Would you consider yourself a suspect?" I asked. "I can arrange to have the sheriff question you, if you'd like."

"No," he said quickly. "It's just that I knew her personally and I'm in from out of town. I assumed that I'd be questioned."

"So, I ask you again, Mr. Wheaton, what do you need to see me for? Go to the sheriff."

"Well, you approached Lanny, so I assumed you wanted to see me as well. I also just wanted to ask what you knew regarding her death and didn't know who else to ask. I apologize if I've wasted your time," he said.

More people walked into the Gaheimer House and Elmer Kolbe, who sometimes assists me with the tours, would come to the door in a few minutes and tell me that the tour was ready to start.

"I'm a friend of the sheriff's," I said. "I can relay your message. Is there something you want him to know? Where you were on Tuesday night and early Wednesday morning, that sort of thing?"

"I was visiting my cousin, Karen. She lives out in St. Peters."

"You weren't with Lanny Lockheart?" I asked, stunned.

"Well . . . yes, I was," he said.

"I thought you were with your cousin?" I asked.

"She was with me . . . us. We were all three together," he answered.

Yeah, right. He was lying and I knew it.

"Victory!" Sylvia snapped from behind me. "It's time for the tour."

"Yes, Sylvia. Be right there," I said over my shoulder. "Mr. Wheaton, what exactly did Lanny say to you?"

"We met for lunch—"

"Why?"

"I'm in town for a convention. We're colleagues."

"Are you a history professor, too?"

"No. My interest is strictly as a hobby. Anyway, we met for lunch and he said that you had come to him and told him that Marie's death was beginning to look like a murder because of a grave robber?"

"Something like that."

"Can I ask what they were looking for?" he asked.

"I'm not privy to say. But I will tell you that a friend of mine was nearly killed because of it."

"Oh, how terrible. What was she doing?"

"Translating," I said before I could stop myself. Oops.

"So it is in French, is it?" he asked more to himself than to me.

"Did I say anything was French?" I asked. "I didn't say what language anything was in. I simply said she was translating."

He looked at me speculatively. Then he began to tug on his bottom lip with his fingers. It came across as a nervous habit.

"Victory! Let's go. People are waiting," Sylvia shouted.

"I have to go, Mr. Wheaton. It was nice talking with you and I'll be sure to have the sheriff speak with you since you're so concerned. He'll be bobbing for apples at two if you want to find him," I said and turned to walk up the steps.

I did not look back at him, but I knew he was staring a hole through me.

A convention of some sort. French documents. Andrew knew that I was referring to French documents before I said anything. He knew what I was talking about. What did it all mean? Why had Lanny lied to me about being with Andrew the night Marie was killed? Andrew switched his answer way to quickly to be telling the truth.

As I walked up the steps of the Gaheimer House to begin the tour, I remembered one thing. I didn't get to ask Andrew if he got to see Marie at all before she died. Sheriff Brooke would remember to, I assured myself.

My tour would suffer from this encounter. There would be no way I could keep my mind on my job. I couldn't wait to get home and look at the translations that Camille had done for me. There were only three, but maybe I could learn something from them.

Fourteen

Papers were piled on my desk, books were in my lap and on the floor. It was one A.M., some twelve hours after I had spoken to Andrew Wheaton. I heard Rudy snoring from the bed and felt a twinge of guilt for keeping him up as late as I did.

I poured the rest of my Dr Pepper into my glass even though the ice cubes had long since melted. I had a pencil behind each ear and one in my hand. I wore only a T-shirt, extra-large of course, and my underwear. I could never have lived in a society before the invention of extra-large T-shirts. For sleeping, nothing beats them.

Fritz had curled himself up under my chair right at my feet. If I was upstairs, he was either in the middle of my bed or at my feet. He was also strategically snuggled so that the light from my lamp on the desk did not hit his eyes. Fritz was a very smart dog.

I began with the first letter. There was no name given to whom the letter was written, just *Countess*. And it was signed only *Antoine*. But between the opening and closing of the letter there were a few names. One was the former Archbishop of Reims. All I had to do was figure out who was Archbishop of Reims in the mid-to-late 1600s. Antoine speaks of him as dying in 1694 so his reign must have been some time before that.

. . . *Henri de Lorraine. The Duc du Guise.* The name jumped off the page in front of me.

I knocked over my desk lamp when I connected the name. It crashed to the floor, pulling the plug out of the wall. Fritz yelped.

"Not now, honey," Rudy said from the bed.

It was dark as pitch and I didn't want to turn on the overhead light, because it was bright and obnoxious. I had no choice. I couldn't get the plug back in the socket by feeling alone. I can't figure out why it is so difficult. You can feel the holes and you have the plug, but it just won't go in. So I turned on the overhead light, and it shone directly into our room, onto the bed, and into Rudy's eyes. He rolled over rather violently and shoved the pillow over his head.

"Sorry," I whispered. I plugged the desk lamp back in and turned off the overhead light. I sat in my chair, listening to it creak, and stared at the book in front of me. Henri de Lorraine, the Duc du Guise, was descended from Charles de Lorraine, who was the heir to the throne of France when Hugh Capet usurped the throne at the end of the tenth century.

Charles de Lorraine was the ancestor of Marie Dijon; I recalled that from her family charts.

Louis XIV was the descendant of Hugh Capet the usurper.

Was this letter in 1756 pointing toward the possibility of overthrowing the French crown?

"Holy cow," I said aloud. "The letter from Antoine says 'his information to use against the crown is intact and somewhere safe.' He was referring to Henri de Lorraine as having information."

107

I drank down the last of my Dr Pepper. "It's too far out," I said. "Why would somebody die for this?"

"I don't know," Rudy answered from the bedroom. "But if you don't stop talking to yourself *I'm* going to commit murder over it."

"Sorry, sweetie," I said.

"It's one in the morning," he went on. "That stuff is two hundred and fifty years old. One more night isn't going to hurt anything. Come to bed."

"Yes, dear," I said. I didn't want to, though. I was on to something. I wanted to stay up all night while my mind was in this mode. But, I thought as I yawned, maybe a good night's sleep would give me a fresh outlook.

And Lanny Lockheart was a history professor.

And Andrew Wheaton referred to it as a "hobby."

Marie was related to the people in this two-hundred-and-fifty-year-old letter.

And somebody dug up her grave looking for this and nearly killed Camille for it.

"Torie!" Rudy pleaded. "My eyes feel pasty. I have to work tomorrow."

"Henri de Lorraine," I said to the photograph in the history book. "We have a date tomorrow." I turned off the table lamp and walked carefully into our bedroom.

Henri de Lorraine must have been imprisoned for what he knew. It was the last thought I had as my head hit the pillow.

•

"I can't seem to find any written documentation that Henri de Lorraine, Duc du Guise, was ever imprisoned," Aunt Bethany Crookshank said to me. She stood behind the counter at the library looking very unlibrarianlike. Her blond hair was turning slightly gray, giving her hair a weird beige look. She was short, trim, and a snappy dresser. She looked quite a bit like her sister, my mother. The same dark eyes and aquiline nose, but blond and a rounder face.

"As a matter of fact," she stated as she pulled her reading glasses off of her nose and let them dangle by their chain, "every source says that he was born in 1614 and died in 1664."

"Fudge," I said. "That can't be. It has to be him that they are referring to."

"Who?" she said.

"The ancient ones," I answered her in a snide tone of voice.

There was nobody else in the library at the moment. It was quiet and overly warm. My face felt hot and I knew that it was probably flushed.

Aunt Bethany reached over and conked me lightly on the head with the book she had in her hand.

"Ouch," I said. "Aunt Bethany, I just got wounded the other day, you know."

"Sorry, forgot," she said. "But you shouldn't get snotty with me because you can't figure out a centuries-old puzzle. Next time I'll hit you with *War and Peace*," she said. "You'll straighten up. Did I ever tell you about how long it took me to find your great-great-great—I think it was three greats—grandpa in the ships' manifests?"

"Five years," I said as she said it.

"Yes, that's right. Hours and hours I would sit, cranking that microfilm reader. That was before they had the electronic ones. All told I probably spent . . ."

"Three hundred and fifty-seven hours."

"Yes, about that. Three hundred and fifty-seven hours looking for one man's name. I can't tell you how gratifying it was when I finally found him."

The thing I like about Aunt Bethany is that she tells the same stories over and over, until I have them memorized. That way I can correct her if she gets anything wrong. It's also a trait that I possess and I like to see that somebody else is just as annoying as me. There's security in numbers.

"So," she went on. "You've only been looking for this duke for a couple of days."

"Couple of hours," I corrected.

"Well, for Pete's sake," she said, "you don't have any reason to be so down about not finding him yet. When you've been looking for him for three hundred and fifty-seven hours, then you can come and complain to me."

"It'll be too late then," I said.

She ruffled my bangs and smiled at me. It was entirely impossible to act or feel like a thirty-three-year-old mother of two around my family. My grandmother swats me on the behind, my mother frets over me eating too much or not eating the right things, Aunt Bethany still ruffles my hair. I suppose she will do that when I'm fifty-seven and she's ninety.

"How have you been?" she asked me. "I see you every day almost, but we don't always talk. Not really talk. Do you ever think about Norah?" she asked me.

Norah was the woman that Sheriff Brooke bought the antiques shop from. It was also the first dead body I had ever encountered outside of a funeral home. Believe me, there's a difference.

"I think of her a lot."

"I hope you try to think of her in a good way," she said. Aunt Bethany was wearing a beige blouse with a big flowery scarf, rich in autumn colors, draped over her left shoulder. She was such a pretty woman. She was divorced and had three children, but those events of her life left no markings on her psychologically or physically. I've had two children and have this nice little bulge below the naval to prove it. Aunt Bethany had no such bulge. And no battle scars from one of the nastiest divorces I've ever heard of.

"You mean, think of her as being alive and not covered in blood," I said. "Yes, I try to think of her the way she was when she came to my office the last time. But sometimes, the other image slips in. You don't have any control over what you're thinking when you're dreaming."

"I hate that," she said.

"Yeah, me, too." I sighed heavily and returned the book I had in my hand back to the shelf. "I don't know what to make of this Duc du Guise guy."

"Well, maybe they made an official statement of some sort announcing his death, but he was actually imprisoned instead."

"I've thought of that. But surely there would be people who witnessed his burial."

"Maybe that was a front, too."

"Why?" It didn't make sense. "I'm beginning to wonder if the documents are a hoax. The people who authored them are lying. But I can't figure out why," I said.

"Or maybe they could be telling the truth and we've been *officially* lied to down through history."

Lord. I didn't need to hang around Aunt Bethany too much. She was more conspiratorial than I was. "You're dangerous," I said to her.

"Just trying to help."

I gave her a kiss on the cheek and a slight hug. "I've got to go," I said. "Thanks for your help."

"Wait a sec," she said. "Where did you say he was imprisoned?"

"I'm not sure. Something about Sainte Marguerite or some female name. Why?"

"I thought I'd try and find something on the prison itself."

"Okay. I'd appreciate it," I said and exited.

Fifteen

I kid you not," my mother said to me. "The mayor is thinking of building a strip mall along the wharf."

"That's ridiculous," I said. "When it floods we can barely save the buildings that are a hundred feet from the river. Much less buildings that would be right on the wharf. Is he nuts?" I didn't really care if I got an answer to that question. I had my own personal opinions of the mayor, and it wouldn't matter if anybody agreed with me or not.

"He claims that he's going to get a new and higher levee put in upriver at Lamont."

"Just hush," I said as I held up a hand. "I don't want to discuss this any further."

We were seated out on the back porch. Mom's current work of art was on the easel. It was a painting of me as a child, looking out of a window. There were small inconsistencies in the painting, but she had captured the spirit. She had captured the life in me. My signature, staring out of the eyes on the canvas. When that was accomplished, it didn't really matter what the rest of the painting was.

The chickens were restless, pecking away at the ground long after any remains of the morning's feed were gone. It was a cool night in early October and the mayor had built a fire. Smoke swirled above his house, trailing into the woods beside our property.

Fritz snoozed under my chair with his long nose resting on the top of my foot. Nobody had come forward to claim him as of yet, and I was getting mighty used to having him around.

"Colin is taking me to see *La Bohème*," she said.

"Puccini? How wonderful."

"I want to say this and I don't want you to get all upset and start talking before I can finish what it is I have to say. Your father does the same thing and it drove me nuts with him the same as it drives me nuts with you."

"Yeah, but you can't divorce me," I said.

She smiled. I'm sure there were times when I was sixteen that she wished she could have divorced me. I wouldn't have blamed her if she had. I was a handful. But she didn't give up on me. That's the great thing about my mother. She never gives up. She might lay low for a while, but she's only regrouping. She is an expert at it. It's like guerrilla warfare for the dysfunctional.

"I hope that you and Colin have set aside your differences."

"Well, yes. I suppose."

"Because I think he plans on sticking around for a time," she said and blushed.

"I guess if I was honest with myself I'd have to say that besides being stubborn and overzealous when it comes to citizens trying to get pregnant women to hospitals, he's an all right guy," I said.

"Gee, thanks," she said. "I think."

Sheriff Brooke was not mean. He was not abusive. He was not a murderer, cheat, thief, or drunkard. The problems that I had with him paled seriously when compared to some of the guys that my mother could be dating.

"No, really," I said. "He's all right. I think we've worked through our trivial skirmish."

"Good," she said. "Because you do tend to blow things out of proportion." She smiled, and her crow's-feet suddenly appeared.

"Yeah, yeah, yeah."

"So are you gonna read that diary Sylvia gave you?" she asked.

"How do you know about it?" I asked.

"Everybody knows about it."

Wilma must have mentioned it to the wrong person.

"Hello?" Sheriff Brooke came from around the side of our house. "Couldn't get an answer at the door," he said.

Fritz looked up from his nap long enough to see if the sheriff was friend or foe. He looked around groggy-eyed and laid his head back on my foot.

"We're just enjoying the October weather," Mom said.

He smiled at her. It was kind of neat to watch. I don't think I could pinpoint what he was thinking or feeling at that moment, but it was the look. It was the look that a man gives a woman and every woman hopes to get. *You are my world.* That's what it said. It didn't say "I love you." That was too easy.

What bothered me was that it came out of nowhere. When did they come to mean this much to each other? Had I been sleeping? Could I not see this growing between them because I was too submersed in my own world? Or was it that I hadn't wanted to see it? Well, I could see it now.

I felt like a Peeping Tom. But, hey, it was my porch.

"Torie," he began. "Got a report on a red Honda Civic seen in Marie's driveway on Tuesday. The witness can't remember what time of day it was, only that it was sometime Tuesday."

"Any idea who it belongs to?"

"Not yet," he said. "But I did run down the inhaler. One Andrew Wheaton got his Proventil refilled at the Rexall in Wisteria. Andrew Wheaton is one of the names on the guest registry of Marie's funeral, and he's staying at the Murdoch Inn."

"Something's funny there," I said. "Lanny Lockheart told me that he was with Andrew the night Marie was killed and that he never got to see Marie. Andrew first said he was with his cousin, and then changed his story. I think he's lying. I think he was alone with his cousin. So why would Lanny give Andrew as his alibi? It's too easy to check. He must have known that Andrew would back him up."

"When did you talk to Andrew?" he asked.

"Sunday at the Octoberfest. That's another weird part. He walked right up to me. I didn't go looking for him," I said.

"Well, we know that Andrew was inside Marie's house sometime before she was killed," he said. "Any luck with the documents?" he asked.

"I haven't even started on the coded one. The letter from the countess is only confusing me even more. I don't know if the content of the papers is what these people are actually after. Because all I have so far is that there once was this duke who was an archbishop and he died," I said. "You tell me that's worth murdering somebody for."

"It must relate to something," he said.

"I'm at a loss," I confessed. "Can I visit Camille yet?"

"Yes, as a matter of fact you can," he said.

"If she's still speaking to me, maybe she can help me figure out what all of this means."

"She doesn't blame you, Torie. You didn't know what you had when you took it to her."

"No. But if I hadn't been so sneaky in the first place . . . well, let's chalk that one up to experience."

The sheriff and my mother were back to looking at each other again, so I grabbed Fritz and went in the house. I was hungry. What else is new? Chili sounded good. I got my biggest pot out of the cabinet and prepared to make one heck of a mess.

I was pulling out the cans of kidney beans when the phone rang. "Hello," I said.

"Hey, baby," Rudy said. "I'll be home kind of late tonight."

"Why?"

"Gotta put up this stupid water heater display," he said. "I wish Tom would stick to faucets and such. They aren't as heavy."

"Okay," I said. "I'm just making chili. That's easy to warm up."

"Good. Well, the other reason I was calling was Amy wanted to know if you would go through your history books and see what you can find for her on the Drudis?" he asked.

"You mean Druids?"

"I suppose. She's doing some paper on heathens or something."

Amy was my husband's youngest sister and she was currently attending Washington University. She often called and made use of my extensive library.

"Sure, I'll pull some books for her. You can take them by

tomorrow on your way to the office or I can take them to her."

"Okay," he said. "I'll see you later. Love you."

"I love you," I said and we hung up.

I pulled out an onion and began chopping it. My eyes burned and huge tears fell and landed on the cutting board. Aah. Good strong onions. If they don't make me cry, I don't want them in my food.

Washington University. Wasn't that where the conference that Lanny Lockheart had said he was attending was supposedly being held? I had forgotten until Rudy mentioned Amy, which made me think of Washington University.

I picked up the phone, thumbed through the yellow pages until I found the university. I called the general information number and a woman answered the phone.

"Yes," I said. "I was wondering if you could give me some information on the conference that you are hosting there this week?"

"A conference?" she asked.

"Or a convention. It should have something to do with history or theology or . . . something," I said. Boy did I sound brilliant.

"Hold on a minute," she said.

The smell of onions was strong on my hand that held the phone. I waited for maybe a minute and a half.

"I'm sorry," she said. "We are not hosting a convention this week on any of our grounds."

"You're sure? What about last week?"

"No, ma'am. There is nothing scheduled in the way of a conference or a convention for the entire first quarter."

"Well, okay," I said.

Hmm. Lanny had lied about Andrew being with him the

night of Marie's death, I was almost certain. Now he was lying about the convention. Or maybe there *was* a conference, just not at Wash U. Why wouldn't he want me to know where the convention was?

Probably because I would try and go, I decided.

Sixteen

The weekends of the Octoberfest are when we hold all of our contests. During the week the town still has the bluegrass festival and the rides and plenty of food. But a lot of our town has to go back to school and back to regular jobs during the week so we don't have as many fun events.

It was Thursday. I was standing across from Pierre's Bakery, looking at Marie's house. The police tape was wrapped around it in some macabre imitation of a big yellow bow. "Tie a Yellow Ribbon" was the song that came to my mind.

I had promised Sheriff Brooke that I would not step foot on Marie's property and I wouldn't. I was just standing there, trying to get an idea of who had a good view of her house. Obviously, Pierre's and the firehouse were the places in view.

I could smell Pierre's before I ever walked in the door. Once inside, the sweet smell of a dozen different breads and pastries and the glorious aroma of fresh-brewed coffee and tea were heavier than on the street. And nearly more than mortal man could take, I might add. The place was full of tourists, and Joe had a smile that went from ear to ear. He managed to look up at me and wave. I waved back and waited in line.

Pierre's is owned by the man behind the counter, Joseph

Frioux. Coziness is Pierre's selling point. Small tables are fit snugly in the dining area, each one with a pink tablecloth and its own china tea set. There's a teapot, coffeepot, sugar, creamer, and matching cups and saucers for each table. The tea and coffee are complimentary. Joe prices the breads and pastries high enough to cover it.

But like any good business owner in a tourist town, there is also a carryout line.

"Hey, Joe," I said when it was my turn.

"Torie, how ya doin'?"

"Fair to partly cloudy," I answered.

"What can I getcha?"

"I'll order in a minute. I was wondering if we could talk?"

"Sure," he said. "Dooley, come take over the counter," he yelled.

Joe is a few years older than me. He has a long face with a very long nose. The fact that he is bald only adds to the length of his face. He has kind blue eyes and a dark, thick mustache that is almost a Fu Manchu, but not quite.

The man who came to take over the counter was older, probably about seventy-five, and I was instantly struck by the fact that I did not know who he was. I'd never seen him before. Except at Marie's funeral.

"Who is that?" I asked.

"Dooley? Well, his name is Ransford Dooley, but I'll be damned if I'll call him Ransford. Can you just imagine it? 'Hey, Ransford, come and help the customers.' Nah, it sounds like he should be a butler or something. Dooley sounds better."

We sat down at a table, and Joe poured me a cup of tea with a generous teaspoon of sugar. Exactly like I take it. Joe is good at his job.

"Thank you," I said. I watched him pour himself a half a cup of coffee and fill the rest of his cup with cream.

"It's what I call half and half," he said. "Hey, is Rudy going to be able to make it bowling next week? I noticed that he missed this past week."

"Yeah, he was at a plumbing convention. Thrills, thrills," I said. "Look, the reason I'm here is . . ." I pointed across the street as I spoke. "I noticed that you've got a real good view of Marie Dijon's house. Did you notice anything unusual going on over at her house or did you see anything the night she died?"

"Well, let me see, Mr. Holmes," Joe said with a fake English accent. "I believe it was half past four on the evening of . . ." He broke into laughter, and I kicked him under the table. "Ouch, I'm just joking," he said.

"Well, I'm serious."

"No, I didn't see anything the night she died. I will say that there was an awful lot of traffic going on over there a few days prior to that Tuesday," he said. "Cars in and out. There was a lot going on."

"Did you see any of the people?" I asked. "Males? Females?"

"Didn't pay any attention," he said. "Dooley might have, though."

"Who is he?" I asked. "The only time I can recall seeing him was at Marie's funeral. Does he live around here?"

"He moved here about a year ago. He and Marie were sweet on each other," he said.

The tea scalded the back of my throat when he said that because I gulped it instead of sipped it. "Really?"

"Yeah. She'd come over here and sit for hours and they'd flirt. It was good for Dooley. That was part of the reason that she was found when she was."

"Why?"

"Because Dooley hadn't seen her in a few days and that was totally unlike her. I mean if nothing else, I make a really good rye bread that she just couldn't live without. But Dooley kinda got worried, 'cause he said that once he got to thinking about it, he hadn't seen her check her mail or anything else. So he went over to see about her and sure enough, she was at the foot of her stairs," he said.

"Oh."

Ransford Dooley looked over at our table as if he knew that we were speaking about him. What a twist this was. Marie and this man sweet on each other. Suddenly I wanted to know more about Mr. Dooley.

"Thanks for the tea, Joe. I've got to go. If you think of anything specific about that week that Marie died, give me a call," I said as I stood up.

"Sure will. Tell Rudy I'll give him a call later this week."

"Okay, and oh—have two loaves of that rye bread sliced and I'll come by and get it in about an hour."

"Certainly."

As I stepped outside I noticed two people stood across the street having a very intense conversation. I recognized one of those people. It was Eleanore Murdoch. I also knew the back of the person she was speaking to but couldn't place it. Then she turned her face slightly and looked over at me. It was Yvonne Mezalaine.

Oh, God. The last thing I or anybody in this town needed was for Eleanore to get involved with Yvonne Mezalaine. I didn't trust Yvonne. I didn't believe that she was Marie's half sister. Somebody recording their family tree didn't usually leave off siblings because of a family feud. You may not speak to a person ever again, but you still put their name on the records. It was interesting the way she slipped up at Wilbert's office and said that Marie's pedigree was impressive, when it would have been hers as well. Why hadn't she said *my* family tree?

I crossed the street and decided to save them from one another. I wasn't sure who could do more damage to whom.

"Eleanore," I said, "how nice to see you."

"Torie, hello," she said. She looked me up and down and finally settled on my face. She had a habit of doing that. There wasn't much to look at where I was concerned. The majority of my wardrobe consisted of jeans and shirts. I owned a few dresses and maybe two nice pants outfits and some shorts. But jeans usually cut it. Maybe that was her polite way of telling me that I dressed like a slob.

"Ms. Mezalaine," I said in acknowledgment. "How are you ladies today?"

"Just fine," Eleanore said.

"I was just leaving," Yvonne said. "Good day, Mrs. Murdoch. Remember what I said earlier." She turned to me then. "Mrs. O'Shea." She then walked away, shoulders thrown back and looking like a million bucks.

I must have stared after her for a good solid minute. Was it something I said?

"Thanks a lot, Torie," Eleanore said. Her earrings were big pieces of plastic fruit that clanged together. I don't know how she could hear herself talk.

"What were you two talking about?" I asked.

"If you must know, I'm conducting my own investigation of the Marie Dijon murder."

"What?!"

Eleanore physically leaped when I yelled. The reason that I didn't ask her anything more intelligent than that was because I was too angry to formulate a coherent question.

"Yes. Did you know that Yvonne is Marie's sister? And that Dooley, over at Pierre's, was having an affair with her?"

"They were sweet on each other. Why does everything have to be so illicit with you?"

"I am not illiterate," she announced.

"Ugh," I moaned.

"Do you want to know what I think?" she asked.

"No. I don't."

"I think you are jealous. I think you are worried that I will solve the mystery before you," she said.

"What . . . wait . . . this is . . ." I couldn't talk.

"I have exterminated every piece of evidence thoroughly," she said.

"Examined. You've examined the evidence."

"Yes. I'm not being careless, you know. You just don't like me horning in on your territory. Well, let me tell you, Victory O'Shea, what's good for the chicken is better for the rooster."

"Oh, Eleanore. If you're going to be profound, at least try to be correct about it." But I knew what she was getting at. If I could be nosy and conduct an investigation, so could she. And to say that she couldn't would be rather conceited. And selfish.

"What's more, I followed Mr. Wheaton and Mr. Lockheart into St. Louis the other day," she went on as I began to get sick to my stomach.

"What . . . you *what?*"

"Yes. They went to Cervantes. The convention center."

"They did?"

"Yes. And I'm not telling you anything more, or you'll try and take credit for it."

"Wait. I've been meaning to speak to you about what you printed about Sylvia," I said, proud of myself for getting out a complete sentence.

125

"What about it? Great interrogative reporting, was it not?" she said. It was clear that she was pleased.

"You have set Sylvia off her course," I said. "She's very upset. I don't know where you got your information, but you shouldn't have printed something like that. You should never have speculated."

"Yvonne is the one that told me about Sophie Gaheimer," she said.

Yvonne? Hold everything. This was too weird. Eleanore had run that article just after Marie's body was found. Nobody except me had speculated that Marie had been murdered. It was safe to say that Eleanore wouldn't have been investigating Marie's murder at that stage of the game. So what reason would she have to speak to Yvonne on the subject of Sophie Gaheimer? On *any* subject, for that matter. Did Yvonne come to her with the information? But why?

Maybe Eleanore was just yanking my chain and she really got the information somewhere else.

A few seconds later I looked up to ask Eleanore how she knew Yvonne, but she was gone. She was headed east in the direction of the river.

Seventeen

I was reading. Silently, by myself. A wonderful autumn breeze blew in my office window as evening approached. I had set aside my history books and started reading Hermann Gaheimer's diary. My run-in with Eleanore and what she said about Sophie had made me very curious.

Hermann Gahiemer arrived in this country from Germany in the 1860s. He married Sophie in 1874. They had no children for nearly ten years. In March 1883 Hermann wrote this entry in his diary:

> Sophie is pregnant and I know it is not mine for I cannot father children. She thinks I am ignorant of the truth. But it so happens that it is she who is ignorant. For I never told her that I could never have children of my own . . .

Hmm. Hermann made a vague reference to having had scarlet fever when he was younger. I assumed that was what had rendered him sterile. Some ten years later the journal speaks of Sophie's lover being Gaston Levaldieu and that all three of their children are his. But all three have the name Gaheimer. He goes on to say in an even later entry that Sophie's lover cannot be trusted, that he saw him speaking to a man of questionable character.

Intrigued, I continued reading. For the next thirty-five years Hermann only mentions his work, the town, and politics, and he does mention the children that he was raising as if they were his own. But around 1920 he begins to mention Sylvia. He speaks of her as being the most beautiful thing alive. When he first saw her he thought she was an angel and then he thought she was a devil because he did not think that God could create something as perfect and enchanting as she was.

It's not long before his diary begins to tell of their shared love and I tried to skip through it as much as possible. Somehow I felt, once again, that I was a Peeping Tom, peeking across time. Then came this entry:

> Sophie cares not that I love Sylvia. To divorce Sophie would be a scandal for Sylvia. I cannot do that to her. The children are grown and I've told them the truth, that I am not their father. I have left them each a small cash settlement in my will, with the provision that, if they contest it, I leave them nothing.

It was a reminder of the shrewd businessman that Hermann Gaheimer had been. Sylvia learned everything she knew from him. Finally, the last entry dealing with Sophie:

> Truly a dark day. Sophie is dead. She was pushed to her death. I know, because I saw it happen. I will let him get by with murder, because Sophie deserved it. For her betrayal and her horrible twists of truths, she deserves what she got. Lord have mercy on my demented soul. . . .

Wow. Hermann Gaheimer never ceased to amaze me. Sophie was pushed and Hermann never told a soul. The few people that were told the particulars of her death were told she had committed suicide. It must have been his final revenge on her—telling everybody she had taken her own life, even though the papers said it was an accident.

"Oh, my God!" I heard Rudy yell from the bedroom. "Quick, Torie. Hurry!"

I dropped the diary and ran into the bedroom and stopped at the doorway. Now, Rudy is a very brave man. He is strong in character and body. But he has one weakness, one very large phobia, and it just so happens to be mine as well.

Spiders.

Rudy had one foot on the edge of our bed and the other foot on the top of the dresser so that he was not touching the floor at all. In his hand was a baseball bat. Between his legs on the floor was a wolf spider the size of a large jawbreaker. His legs were the size of small branches. Okay, that might have been an exaggeration, but he was huge!

"Kill him," he said in a flat voice.

"You kill him," I said back to him.

"I'm not killing him."

"Well, I'm not killing him either," I argued. "As soon as I head toward him, he'll run under the bed. I'd rather stand here and look at him all night than have to go to bed knowing he's alive."

"Well, do something," he said.

"What do you suggest? Why don't you just jump on him?"

"Because I'll miss and he'll run up my leg and you'll be a widow."

Rachel and Mary came scrambling up the steps and stopped dead in the doorway. "Wow," Rachel said. "He's huge."

"Huge?" Rudy asked. "He's big enough to give a name."

"Okay," I said. "How about some Raid. Do we have any Raid?"

"No," he said. "You won't allow any poisonous chemicals in the house because you don't want us all to get cancer. Remember?"

"Well," I said, "the next time we go to the store and I tell you that you can't buy any bug spray, buy it anyway!"

In the meantime the spider remained calm and cool and never moved an inch. It was rather polite of him to allow us to have this argument.

"My teacher says to use hair spray," Rachel said.

"Hair spray?" I asked.

"Yeah, she says it will stiffen them."

"I want it dead, Rachel. Not tortured. Besides, I don't think we have any hair spray either."

"Why don't you just step on him?" Rachel asked.

"Because," I said, "it scrunches and it feels like I'm crushing bones or something. It gives me the heebie jeebies."

The spider moved.

"George," Rudy said to it. "You stay right there, George."

Rachel and I shrieked. Mary, however, walked over very calmly and smashed George the Spider. Just like that. No squealing or cringing. No hesitation. Just splat and he was dead.

"Don't you feel like an idiot?" Rudy said to me.

"No. You're the one with the baseball bat."

"Am I interrupting something?" Aunt Bethany said from behind.

"Oh, no," I said. "We were just killing a spider."

"It takes the whole family?" she asked.

"It takes this whole family," I answered.

Rudy got down from his safety and came over and kissed Aunt Bethany on the cheek. "Hi, beautiful," he said.

"Hello, ugly," she said back to him.

"I'm going downstairs to get a snack," Rudy said. "Torie, will you pick George up and give him a proper burial?"

"I'm not picking him up," I said. "You pick him up. You were his intended victim."

"No, you pick him up," he said as he headed down the steps. Even dead, spiders were a menace.

"I've got some news for you," Aunt Bethany said.

"Great."

Rachel and Mary were hanging on Aunt Bethany's legs. It was a good thing I didn't have three children. There wouldn't be any room for the third one to wallow.

"Girls, get off her," I said.

Aunt Bethany squeezed them back. "I just love your girls," she said to me. "My girls are going through that weird teenage stuff."

Her oldest child, Adam, is twenty-two. The twins, Lara and Lynn, are now fifteen. Girls going through teenage metamorphosis are quite different from boys.

"I try to remember that all adults were teenagers once, and we survived," she said.

I laughed at that one. "So, what kind of news did you say you had?"

"Sainte Marguerite," she said. "It's the island of Sainte Marguerite."

"Yeah? What about it?" As soon as I asked, I knew what about it. "Oh, my God. *The* island of Sainte Marguerite."

"What's an island?" Mary asked.

"It's a country with water around it," Rachel answered her.

Aunt Bethany had never stopped staring at me. I stared back as the implications of this hit home.

"The man in the iron mask," I whispered.

She nodded.

"Oh, my God," I repeated as the gooseflesh rose on my arms. "Nah, no way. Oh, my God." I wasn't sure on the particulars but I knew that the man in the iron mask was an actual prisoner held in France, not just a work of fiction.

I shoved some books off my desk, rummaging around to find the letter to the countess. "Listen to this," I said to my aunt. " 'The rumor of Louis XIV having a twin brother at birth, is but that . . . a rumor. In 1694 I was called to the island of Sainte Marguerite.' Wow. See, her cousin had died and was replaced by his valet who died at the Bastille in 1703. Holy cow!"

"The man in the iron mask was imprisoned in 1664 and died in 1703."

"Who was the man in the iron mask?" I asked.

"Nobody knows," she said. "Alexander Dumas liked to think that it was a twin brother to Louis XIV."

"What?" I asked the question but I don't physically remember moving my mouth.

"Yes. See, the legend says that a seer told the king that his wife would give birth to twin boys and that they would tear apart the kingdom fighting over who should be king," she explained. I looked perplexed I'm sure, so she went on. "Back then twins were a real dilemma. Their logic was that the first one born was the last one conceived, and that the last one born was the first one conceived. So who should rule? The actual firstborn, or the actual first one conceived?"

"I can see how that would be a problem."

"So, according to the legend, the king and his wife, Anne of

Austria, had the second-born child sent away to live with distant family or somebody, I'm not sure who it was. This child supposedly was never allowed to see a painting or coin with the prince's face on it. According to the legend that Dumas weaves, the exiled prince finds out who he is and tries to overthrow the crown, and he is put in a mask and jailed so that nobody will know who he is."

"Well, but this letter plainly states that particular version as being a rumor. So, let's assume this letter is correct. It is saying that Henri de Lorraine, Duc du Guise, was the man in the mask. Why? Who was the prisoner really? What I mean is, do historians have a *real* theory on who he was?"

"All kinds," Aunt Bethany said. "Everybody from the Duke of Buckingham in England to Vermandois the Grand Admiral of France. Even Molière was considered."

"The guy who wrote *Tartuffe*? That Molière?"

"Yes, that Molière," she said. "Oliver Cromwell, the Duc du Guise, and Nicholas Fouquet. Fouquet is the one I would have picked," she said.

"Wow."

"Yes, wow."

"The documents have to be a hoax," I said.

"Why?"

"It's just not possible," I explained. "Why would Marie be the only person in the world to be keeper of a secret like that?"

"Mom," Rachel said. Her clear, young voice brought me out of my information-overload state of mind. "Can we have a drink?"

"Yes, sweetie. Go down and ask your grandma for one or ask Dad."

Rachel and Mary disappeared down the steps to go get their drinks. I was silent for a while.

"It would explain why somebody would be willing to kill for these papers," Aunt Bethany said.

"What do you mean?"

"Think about it. If you have undeniable proof as to who the man in the iron mask was, it would have to be worth lots of money. Plus a Pulitzer or something like it. It could make somebody's career."

"Lanny Lockheart," I said. "There has to be more to it than that. Marie was related to this man, this Duc du Guise. Maybe she and Lanny had plans to do something with this information. Some sort of joint project."

"But he killed her instead? Is that what you're saying?"

"I'm just throwing out ideas. One thing's for certain," I said. "If Eleanore could follow Lockheart and Wheaton to the Cervantes Convention Center undetected, it would definitely be possible for Mr. Lockheart to have followed me to Camille's."

"And if you're right, they have the papers."

"Yeah. So why are they sticking around? Why haven't they gotten out of Dodge? See? That's what makes me think that there is more to it."

Then I remembered the key that was in the envelope with the documents. I hadn't taken it to Camille's, and I had no idea what it was the key to. It was a skeleton key, so I knew that it would not fit a safety deposit box. Could this be what they were sticking around for?

"Do you think that Camille realized what you had?"

"I think she knew that this letter meant something. I think that, being French, she recognized the name Sainte Marguerite. But I don't think she had any idea of the scope of this," I said.

"So, what next?" Aunt Bethany asked.

"I'm going to need to find out why the Duc du Guise would be considered a threat to Louis." I picked up the other letter that Camille had translated for me. It mentioned an heir and the location of something. The only names were Philippe, somebody named Sauniere, and then who the letter was from: Gaston.

Gaston.

"Torie, what is it?" Aunt Bethany asked. "You just turned sort of gray."

"Gaston?" I asked. I flipped open Hermann Gaheimer's diary. Sophie's lover was Gaston Levaldieu. Sophie died in 1922. The letter written to Philippe from Gaston was written in December 1922. "I think that Sophie Gaheimer's lover is the author of this second letter that Camille translated for me."

"That Marie had?"

"Yes. That might explain why Marie came to live here. Something happened here that connects this whole thing."

"In New Kassel?" she asked.

"Yes." I walked over to one of my bookcases and took out an atlas. I slammed it down on my desk, on top of all of the other books and papers and candy wrappers already inhabiting it.

"What?" Aunt Bethany asked. "What are you looking for?"

"Well, the first time I read this letter from Gaston, something puzzled me. The second line says 'Indeed it is pertaining to 35–40 and 90–95.' I couldn't figure out what he was talking about," I said. I ran my finger over the page. "Bingo!"

"What?"

"Missouri's location on the globe is between 35 and 40 degrees latitude and 90 and 95 degrees longitude."

"Yeah?"

"I don't know. I haven't got the foggiest idea what it means. But I'm onto something."

Eighteen

You're talking complete Greek," Sheriff Brooke said.

We were driving along Highway I-55, headed north to Camille's house. We were in his squad car and he was decked out in his sheriff's uniform, for once. A pair of those dark sunglasses so commonly used by the Highway Patrol were perched on his nose. He was a rather imposing figure in complete dress.

"I know I'm talking Greek."

"You really think that something happened at New Kassel seventy-five or so years ago that pertains to Marie's murder?"

"I'm positive. But I'll be darned if I know what it is. I think maybe this Gaston guy came to New Kassel, what for I don't know. Maybe it was just a small out-of-the-way town, and he thought it would give him anonymity. Anyway, he arrives in New Kassel and he either leaves something here or does something that Marie comes looking for ninety years later."

"Only it gets her killed," he said as he turned on his blinker.

"Yeah, because she's not the only one looking for it."

"So you think that the documents are what she found?"

"I have no blooming idea," I said.

"Well, guess what?"

"What?"

"Your Lanny Lockheart drives a red Honda Civic."

"So he did see her before she died. He lied to me."

"Yeah, and we know Andrew was also in the house before she died because he left the inhaler there."

"What about the car that ran me off the road?"

"We haven't turned up anything other than that it was stolen. No prints or anything. They must have worn gloves," Brooke said.

"Well, I know that the driver wasn't Lanny Lockheart. The driver wasn't that big or heavy. Lanny is a bear of a man. He wouldn't have been able to disappear as quickly as the driver did."

We pulled along the street and parked. I rang Camille's door and waited. Her dark eyes sparkled the minute she saw me. "Torie, Torie, come in."

She hugged me and I could feel how thin she was. She looked to Sheriff Brooke.

"This is Sheriff Brooke," I said. "He's a friend of mine and he wouldn't let me come alone. He's very worried about me."

"Sheriff, please come in."

She led us into the dining room, where coffee and muffins waited. I didn't drink coffee, but I said nothing. I knew Camille, she'd jump up and fix me tea, and I didn't want her going to any extra trouble for me.

"Camille, I am so sorry—"

"Shh. Nonsense," she said. "You had no idea. It's all right. See? I am alive."

"Barely," I said. "I just feel so awful."

"Well, thank you for the flowers," she said. "When they arrived at the hospital, it just made my day."

She set about pouring coffee and handing out muffins. Real butter sat on a sterling silver tray, with a large silver knife beside it.

"I hope you like raspberry muffins," she said.

"I've never had them before," I said. "But my taste buds like anything that is fattening. Cholesterol and fat must have a certain taste to it, and I love it."

The muffins were still warm and they literally fell apart in your mouth. They were scrumptious. The sheriff and I moaned and ooed and moaned some more. Camille was pleased that we liked them.

"Camille, I was wondering if you could help me with a little bit of French history," I said.

"Of course," she said.

"I figured out that the letter to the countess that you translated for me refers to the island of Sainte Marguerite."

"Yes?"

"The island where the man in the iron mask was kept," I said.

"Oh, my," she said. "That's correct."

"Yes, and it mentions the Duc du Guise."

"It does? I don't recall that."

"Well, the Archbishop of Reims at the time of Louis the Fourteenth's reign was Henri de Lorraine, the Duc du Guise."

"I'm impressed, Torie. It would have taken me quite a while to figure that out," she said.

"Well, I was wondering if you would know any reason that Henri de Lorraine would be a threat to Louis? Enough for Louis to have him imprisoned?"

"Are you suggesting that Henri de Lorraine was the identity of the man in the iron mask?" she asked, eyes wide.

"Maybe. I don't know, really. That's why I was wondering if there was a reason that he would have been imprisoned?"

"I don't recall," she said. "But then, I don't remember my history that well. Some of it is very vivid. But not all of it."

"You remember what those documents said, though—the ones you translated?" I asked.

"Only bits and pieces, Torie. They were very complicated."

I was crestfallen. Sheriff Brooke was busy looking around Camille's dining room. An elegant home is awe-inspiring when you first enter it. She liked to decorate with historic flavor, as her copy of the painting, "Queen Guinevere's Maying," by John Collier, showed. So did the medieval engravings on the oppo-site side of the room, and the tapestry of a knight on horseback that hung behind us.

"Camille, did you get a look at the guy that grabbed you the other day?" the sheriff asked.

"No. He was strong, I know that. I turned to run as soon as I heard the door burst open. I tried to run down the hall, but he grabbed me from behind and shoved me through my house and out the back door toward the garage," she explained. Shivers overtook her at the memory of it. "I was so scared."

Guilt. Guilt. Guilt.

"I'm so sorry," I said again.

"Could I get another look at your garage?" Sheriff Brooke cut in.

"Why, certainly," Camille said.

We had finished our muffins and I really wanted another one but wouldn't embarrass myself by asking for it. Since we were finished, we headed out the back door and toward the garage. She opened it and we filed in.

The glass was broken out of one of the windows where

Camille had tried to get out. Her blue Saturn sat in the middle of the room, with shelves on one wall filled with tools and such. A weed whacker was leaning up against the door frame. I don't know what I was expecting. I just knew that I was relieved that there wasn't any blood. Don't ask me where I thought the blood was going to come from. I was just relieved that there wasn't any.

Sheriff Brooke walked around the car with much deliberation.

"Have you driven it since the incident?" he asked. She had been home three days. Her car looked like new, even though I knew that she had owned it for several years. She was retired and she did very little driving. Nearly everything she wanted was within walking distance in the Central West End.

"My neighbor brought me home from the hospital. I drove it once to the park. I haven't felt much like going anywhere."

"Forest Park?" he asked.

"Yes."

"That's only a few blocks," he said.

"Correct. I said I haven't felt like going out much."

"What I'm getting at is that your car has half a tank of gas."

"Yes."

"Then your car couldn't have run out of gas the other day during the attack."

She started laughing. "You mean it stalled?" she asked. "It died?" She laughed some more. "You mean because I need a tune-up, I'm alive?"

I found myself smiling from ear to ear. Sheriff Brooke however was not.

"Either that," he began, "or your assailant stuck around."

"Meaning?" I asked.

"Camille," he said, "about how long did it take you to pass out?"

"Not long. Just a few minutes after I broke the window."

"Do you remember hearing if your attacker left the property?" Sheriff Brooke asked.

"I couldn't tell," she said. "I just assumed he did."

"What?" I asked Sheriff Brooke. "What?"

"Well, I'm wondering if the assailant didn't stick around, wait till she had passed out but wasn't dead. Then he came in and turned off her engine."

"Why?" I asked.

"Maybe he didn't want to kill her. Just like he might not have intended to kill Marie."

"Marie?" Camille asked.

"So, maybe he only wanted it to *look* like he wanted Camille dead."

"Why?" I asked.

"Why?" Camille echoed.

"Maybe to scare you," he said.

"I don't know. That's pretty far-fetched," I said. "Besides, the doors were locked. How did he get into the car to turn it off?"

"Marie who?" Camille asked again.

"Maybe he had a shim with him to unlock the door," Sheriff Brooke said. "I suppose the car could have just died."

"It seems much more logical," I said.

"But I can't help but speculate—"

"What the hell are you two talking about?" Camille yelled.

"Oh," I said. "The friend who found the documents in the first place. Marie Dijon."

"Marie Dijon? I was at her funeral. Nobody said anything about her being murdered. Are you saying she was murdered?" Camille asked, her rising hysteria evident.

"It looks that way," Sheriff Brooke said.

"*Juste ciel!*" Camille said. She raised her hand to her forehead and then didn't know what to do with it once it got there. "I don't feel so well."

"I don't blame you," I said. "Let's go back in the house, Sheriff. We should be going."

We walked Camille back to her house. We moved quickly as if each of us were afraid the boogeyman was going to jump out at us. The sheriff and I wasted no time. We headed for the front door and prepared to leave.

"I am so sorry, again," I said to Camille. "Please forgive me."

"You are forgiven," she said. "Don't fret, please."

"It's just that we have been friends for quite some time. I hope that you won't think I meant you harm."

"Of course not," she said, and meant it. "You and the sheriff be careful."

"We will," I said.

Nineteen

I sat in my office at the Gaheimer House. It was heading toward evening and I hadn't even considered going home yet. Tomorrow was Saturday and I'd have to give four tours instead of the two that I gave on weekdays during the Octoberfest.

My freshly poured Dr Pepper fizzled in my glass. I could hear myself breathe, it was so quiet. Sylvia and Wilma had gone home. I was alone.

I thumbed through the tabs on the files in the top drawer of my file cabinet. This cabinet contained the family charts of all the residents of New Kassel, past and present. Unless, of course, someone didn't want their charts on file.

I laid Marie's on the desk and turned back for Hermann Gaheimer's charts. I wondered if Sylvia knew that Hermann's three children were not his children at all. Would she have bothered to put a family group chart on file for them if she had known?

The first chart listed Hermann's vital statistics as well as his wife's. Then it listed all three of the children, their marriage information, and their children, the date and places of their births and deaths, if they'd died. The oldest child was John Henry Gaheimer, who married Cynthia Webb, and their two daughters were Elizabeth Mary Gaheimer and Vera Catherine Gaheimer, who married Thomas Dooley and Marvin Hackett. It was amazing. They all had the last name Gaheimer when it should have been Levaldieu.

Then I realized what it was I had found. Dooley. Elizabeth had married Thomas Dooley. I flipped the page to see her descendants. She had seven children; the first six were girls and the last one was one Ransford Charles Dooley, born 1924.

Okay, now that I had found it, what exactly did it mean?

It meant that Marie was flirting with the grandson of Gaston Levaldieu, who just happened to be the author of one of the documents that Marie had. Did she know who Ransford was? Did Ransford know who she was? Just who the hell was Marie Dijon anyway? It was obvious that she had a history that I couldn't begin to fathom.

I took a drink of soda and nearly spilled it when the phone rang. I answered it on the first ring. "Hello?"

"I'm sorry, I have the wrong number," the person said, and hung up.

"Thanks a lot," I said to the phone. "You scared the pee out of me."

I had looked at Marie's family charts before. But, I have to admit, before I was looking at them for the ancestry, not the descendants.

Marie's parents were Philippe Jaillard and Henriette Billet. Their children were listed as Jeanne C. Jaillard born 1938, Marie T. Jaillard born 1940, and Dorothee L. Jaillard born 1945. It did not give information on their spouses, but I knew that Marie had married Auguste Dijon. So? What was the catch?

I flipped the page and went back further. Philippe Jaillard's mother was a Levaldieu. So, Marie and Ransford were related. But I asked myself again, did she know that? Thinking about it,

I was also fairly certain that Marie's father Philippe Jaillard was the Philippe that Gaston Levaldieu had written to.

Great. I had it solved. But what in God's name did it mean?

Then something occurred to me. I would bet that Yvonne Mezalaine was either related to or a friend of or somehow connected to Ransford Dooley. It would explain how Eleanore Murdoch found out about Sophie Gaheimer's suicide. Sophie was Ransford's grandmother, after all.

Again, what did it mean? Why would Marie die for this?

I picked up the phone and dialed the sheriff's office.

"Sheriff's office, Wisteria."

"Peg," I said, "gimme Colin."

"Just a minute."

I had been on hold for just a few seconds when the sheriff came on the phone. "Brooke."

"Sheriff," I said, "it's Torie."

"Yeah?"

"I think you should pick up and question Ransford Dooley."

"Who?"

"He works at Pierre's, which is right across from Marie's house, I might add. I just figured it out by examining the charts. Ransford and Marie were cousins, removed a few times, but they were cousins. And I think that Ransford was the grandson of the man who wrote one of the letters that Marie had."

"That Camille translated?" he asked.

"Yeah."

"Marie was in possession of a letter that this Dooley guy's grandfather wrote," he said, processing the information.

"Yes. I think the letter was written to Marie's father."

"But the letter didn't really say anything all that important," he said.

"I know. But combined with all of the other documents and letters, maybe the whole package was worth killing for."

"I don't know," he said. "I just can't imagine that somebody dies for a bunch of yellowed, wrinkled pieces of paper. It's not even money."

"Well, whatever. I think you should pick him up and question him. While you're at it, Yvonne Mezalaine is pretty fishy, too."

"Who?"

I explained.

"Well, she's not staying in New Kassel, or even Wisteria for that matter. I don't know where to find her," he said.

"Well, she always manages to be around, somehow."

I heard a creak on one of the floorboards in the hallway. "Sylvia?" I asked. No answer.

"What's the matter?" Sheriff Brooke asked.

"Nothing."

"Bull, I can hear it in your voice. What's wrong?"

I heard the creak again.

"Wilma?"

I never noticed how creepy the Gaheimer House could be when you're in it all alone, toward dusk.

"Do you want me to stay on the line while you go check it out?" the sheriff said.

"What good will that do me?" I asked. I couldn't help but wonder how he knew that I was hearing something in the house that was scaring me. Could he read my voice that well? "Are you going to shoot somebody over the phone?"

"No."

"Then it won't do me any good if you stay on the line while I go confront my fears," I said. I heard the noise again. "Stay on the line anyway. I'll be right back."

I set the phone down gently and stuck my head out into the hallway. I don't know what I would have done if somebody had been standing there. There was nobody there. But then a frightening thought occurred to me. I would have to walk all the way through the house to get out the door. I suddenly got the creepy sensation that I was being watched.

I darted back to the desk, after I shut the office door and locked it.

"Sheriff?" I asked. I gulped air and tried to get my pulse below 120. "Get over here, right now."

"What is it?" he asked.

"Nothing," I said. "But I am not leaving this office without an escort."

•

"It could have been the ghost of Hermann Gaheimer," Sheriff Brooke said to me in my kitchen.

"Hardy har har," I said.

"Ghost?" Rachel asked, her eyes wide with fear. "Like from a dead person?"

"It's the only kind of ghost that I know of," the sheriff mused.

"Mom," I said, "tell him to quit scaring the kids."

"Colin, quit scaring Torie," my mother said and laughed.

"Fine. You all just pick on me," I said. "I know something or somebody was there. Not only could I hear it, but I got the feeling, you know?"

"What feeling?" Rachel asked. She looked more scared now than before.

"The feeling when you know somebody is there. When you can feel eyes on you."

"Mom, you're scaring me," Rachel said.

"And you were worried about what I said?" the sheriff asked.

"Shut up," I said. "Please, just hush. I can be scared if I want to without feeling guilty about it."

"Of course you can," Rudy said from the hall.

"Hi, sweetie," I answered.

Rudy came over to me and kissed me on the lips. He looked deep into my eyes. His eyes were the perfect color of chocolate. And, oh, how I love chocolate. "You look like you could use a night out."

"I agree," the sheriff said.

"Mom?" Rudy asked. "Would you care to watch the girls tonight while I take my wife out to dinner?"

"Sure," she said.

"And a movie?" he asked me.

For the first time in my life I actually didn't want to go to a movie. I wanted to crawl under my covers and hide until next year. I didn't care if I missed Christmas.

But it was not that often that Rudy asked me out. We went out as the result of me asking him or another couple asking us. He did not extend the invitation himself that often.

"That sounds lovely," I said.

Twenty

From Rudy's point of view, it was a disaster.

"Of all the places I could have picked in New Kassel," he said, "I had to pick Ye Olde Train Depot." He was hiding behind his menu in an effort to be invisible. "I could have picked Frauline Krista's, The Log Cabin, hell, we could have gone to Velasco's for pizza. I even could have taken you in to Arnold for Steak-n-Shake, but no. No. I pick the Train Depot and half of New Kassel is here. The half that we don't want to see, I might add."

He was right. Eleanore and Oscar Murdoch were seated by the fireplace, the mayor and his wife were two tables away, and right smack dab in the middle of the room was a table with none other than Lanny Lockheart and Andrew Wheaton.

"Sorry," I said. Not that it made him feel any better. "We could leave and run over to Velasco's."

"Are you kidding? If we leave after we've been seated it will cause more of a sensation than if we stay. Which, I'll have you know, I am not looking forward to."

Rudy looked really handsome in his salmon pink oxford and navy pants. He even wore a tie. It happened to be his tie with Captain Kirk on it, but it was still a tie. I was dressed in navy pants and a red angora sweater that had red and white sequins around the collar. I was allergic to angora, but I could suffer through the itchy nose and watery eyes the two times a year that I wore this sweater.

"Well, if it makes you feel better," I said, "we have yet to be detected by anybody other than the mayor and his wife. They waved when we first came in. Oh, scratch that. Eleanore just waved."

I gave a little wave to her across the room. Rudy sank farther behind his menu. "Oh, Rudy, put that blasted menu down and act right. You look like a poor James Bond impression."

"Really?" he said and sat up straight. "Poor James Bond is better than no James Bond."

God.

"Now let's just have our dinner and get out of here."

"Sure, you're right. I'm overreacting."

"For once it's you and not me," I said.

Our waiter showed up in his black pants and white pristine shirt. He was as blond as he could be, had hazel eyes, and was quite tall. He looked to be about twenty-three. I think he was finished growing but he had that super-lanky look that goes with youth.

"Hello," Rudy said. "I think I'm going to have the ribs with salad, bread, and steamed vegetables. And iced tea."

"And I'll have the Alaskan snow crab with a baked potato and salad. Bring me a Coke," I said.

Ye Olde Train Depot was exactly that. It used to be the train station back when. After World War II everybody had cars and the train no longer stopped here. Trains still run on the tracks, but they are cargo trains, not passenger trains.

The restaurant had a distinct pre-Depression feel and decoration to it. Elevator music was piped in and people felt more inclined to be extra quiet in this restaurant than in a public library. It wasn't swanky by any means. But it was swanky for New Kassel.

Suddenly the expression on Eleanore Murdoch's face changed. I looked toward the restaurant door.

"You know, honey," Rudy started, "I've been thinking."

"That's good," I said without realizing it. I could see a figure standing in the doorway, but could only get a glimpse of one arm. I was straining to see without outwardly straining, a trick that I'm not sure is possible.

"I think we should take a vacation," Rudy went on. "A long one. Like three or four weeks and let your mom and Colin have the house to themselves."

"Hmm? She can go to his house if she wants."

"But she won't."

I looked to Eleanore to see what she was doing. The same thing I was. Straining to see and yet still carry on a conversation with Oscar. Suddenly the body came the rest of the way into the dining room and walked over to the table that Mr. Lockheart and Mr. Wheaton were seated at.

It was Yvonne Mezalaine.

I knocked over my water glass and caught it on the rebound, spilling maybe a teaspoon of water.

"You're not listening to a word that I'm saying," Rudy said.

"I know. I . . . mean I know it seems that way, but I am."

"You haven't made eye contact with me for the last two minutes."

"I know what your eyes look like, dear," I said.

Rudy looked around the room and found what it was that I was watching. Yvonne gave Andrew a case of some sort. It was smaller than a briefcase, yet larger than the average purse.

Eleanor's eyes got big. So did mine. Then Yvonne left the restaurant as quickly as she came in. "Oh, boy," I said.

"Torie. Torie, you look at me right now."

I complied.

"Now, don't take your eyes off of me. No, no. Don't look away. I know it's hard, Torie. We are having a romantic evening together and that's that."

The elevator music stopped and a spotlight shone on a table at the west end of the room. Amethyst Bradley, the owner of Corner Antiques, was seated on a stool. Her long auburn hair fell over her shoulders like a red river. A snug black gown clung to her perfectly curved figure. Seated next to her was her brother with his guitar. His hair was nearly as long as hers, pulled back into a ponytail. They were voted the most sensual people in New Kassel in my book.

"When did the Train Depot start having music?" Rudy asked.

"They've been having performers for over a year now. You don't get out too much, dear."

"Don't turn around," he said.

"Why?"

"Because you'll turn around to watch the music and really be looking at Eleanore and the sideshow. Now we are going to be romantic if it kills me and we can't be romantic if you're watching Eleanore!"

"Yes, dear," I said. My eyes were watching his when Amethyst began to sing "Desperado." Even her vocal chords were sexy. She sang that song in her breathy alto voice and I thought Rudy was going to bust a blood vessel.

"Hey," I said, "we can't be romantic if you're drooling all over Captain Kirk."

"Sorry."

"Don't sorry me, buster." I flicked my eyes over to Eleanore. "Holy Christ!"

"Jeez, Torie. She's a beautiful woman. I can look. I just can't touch."

"Oh, Jesus, Mary, and Joseph. She's going to steal the briefcase."

"What?" Rudy asked and turned his face in the direction that I was looking.

There was Eleanore in all her glory. She threw her napkin onto the floor and then proceeded to get down on all fours to retrieve it. Amethyst Bradley was the perfect diversion. Lanny and Andrew were watching every breath she took. That could have been because every time she breathed her chest rose in a dazzling display. She even breathed sexy. That didn't seem fair. I wondered what she'd look like having a heart attack.

"Rudy—"

"Don't."

"Rudy, Eleanore is going to get herself killed."

"And your point is?"

"Rudy, I have to stop her."

She snatched the briefcase and was headed to the ladies' room.

"I'm going to go and get that briefcase and put it back on the floor next to Andrew's leg. When I come back into the room, if Amethyst is finished with her son, I'm going to need a diversion."

"And?"

"Well, I'll need you to divert or whatever it's called."

"And just what am I supposed to do? Get up and sing 'Yankee Doodle Dandee'?"

"That's a great idea," I said. "You could do a duet with Amethyst."

I snuck away and headed for the ladies' room. I opened the door and found Eleanore jumping up and down on the briefcase.

"Eleanore!"

She shrieked. "No, you don't," she said. "I got this briefcase all on my own and I'm getting credit for it."

"You're going to get yourself killed, you moron!"

"Moron? Did you call me a moron?"

"Yes, I did, and I can't recall a title ever more deserved!"

Eleanore looked genuinely hurt.

"Did you ever stop to think what it is you're stomping to death? There could be a priceless jewel or a bomb or something in there."

It was clear she hadn't thought of that. Slowly she stepped off of the briefcase and picked it up, snuggling it to her breast.

"Now, listen," I said. "Give me that briefcase and I'll take it out there and return it. I will get you out of this mess, but you have to promise me that you will stop this nonsense right now."

"No."

"Fine. What do you think they're going to do when they realize it's missing? You are dead meat, woman. Now give me the damn briefcase!"

"You don't have to be so mean, Torie. Really, you have the most horrendous manners."

"Well, at least I don't crawl on all fours in a public restaurant and steal people's briefcases."

"I want to see what's inside it," she proclaimed. "Then you can take it back."

I nodded in agreement and she handed me the case. I set it up on the vanity. "Do you have a bobby pin?" I asked.

"No," she said. "I have a safety pin, though." She unhooked it from the inside of her blouse, where it kept the buttons from gapping open.

"I have no idea if this will work or not." I slipped the pointy end into the lock of the case and felt for the lever.

After a good five minutes alternating between cussing at her and stomping my feet, I finally hit it right and it came undone. I know what you're thinking. But God help me, I wanted to see what was in the case as much as she did.

"Where did you learn that?" she asked.

"When I worked at the bank. I kept losing or forgetting my key to my cash box. Finally, my boss said that I was on my own. She wasn't going to let me use the spare key anymore. Voilà. Improvise," I said.

We both looked at each other and held our breath as I lifted the lid. I was going to have a fit if it contained vitamins or something equally innocent. Inside were papers. Flyers and promotional material for some club or society called the Merovee Knights. Meetings were scheduled all across the country, with one in St. Louis at the convention center last week.

"This is what they are all in town for," I said aloud. "And what do you want to bet Marie was a member or something along that line."

"What does it mean?" Eleanore said.

"Hmm?" I needed to watch what I said when I talked to myself. I never knew who would be listening in. "I don't have any idea."

I shut the case. Nobody could tell that the lock had been tampered with. But there were large footprints all over it. I dampened a paper towel and wiped off the foot marks.

"Really, Eleanore. An elephant couldn't have done more damage."

"How are you going to get it back to the table?" she asked.

"Don't worry about it. You just go back to your table and finish your dinner. And I mean it. Keep your nose out of this!"

Her nose went promptly in the air. I'm sure she'd never been more insulted. I didn't care.

I walked out into the dining room and stopped. I waited until Rudy saw me and I nodded to him. Suddenly he jumped up with his hands at his throat coughing and sputtering. If I hadn't known better, I would have sworn he was choking. He was even turning purple.

Everybody in the room stood, some moved in closer, and a brave few actually went to him. I walked quickly to Mr. Lockheart's table and set the case down. Being short has its advantages. Nobody detected me.

At that moment Rudy flung himself backward. I think he intended to land on the floor but misjudged and hit a table, knocking it and the contents onto the floor and all over him.

"Oh, my God!" I yelled. I ran to him like the distraught wife that I would be if it were real. "Oh, God!"

Brett Stuckmeyer, the owner of the place, and our waiter were pounding the living daylights out of Rudy. "I'm fine," he said. "I'm fine."

I rushed to his side. "Rudy, are you all right?"

"Yes," he said, glaring at me. "When the soufflé hit my head and the table hit my back, it must have jarred loose whatever was in there." He was not happy. But a man with soufflé on his face had every right not to be happy.

I looked around the room. Everybody stared at us. I hadn't really expected anything else.

"Let me buy you dinner," I heard Brett say to Rudy.

"No, no. I think we're finished with dinner," he said to him.

I looked to Eleanore who gave me the thumbs-up sign. Mr. Lockheart and Mr. Wheaton glared at me when I got around to making eye contact with them. Then I realized why they didn't look very pleasant. I had returned the case to the wrong chair.

It was suppose to be next to Andrew's chair and I set it next to Lanny's. Oops.

"I think they know," I said to Rudy.

"Probably," he said. He couldn't look more angry if he tried.

"Romantic evening," he quipped. "Huh."

"Well, adventure is better than romance," I said. I tried desperately to justify the soufflé on his face. "Look at it this way. Now Captain Kirk has some soufflé and some wine to go along with your drool."

He growled.

Twenty-one

I didn't tell you to have a seizure, for crying out loud!" I yelled.

"Oh, no, you just wanted me to sing 'Yankee Doodle Dandee'!"

"I never said that."

My mother was at the kitchen table with a glass of milk and a stomach pill. "So I take it you guys didn't go to a movie?"

I glared at her.

"Oh, no," Rudy said. "We *were* the movie! It was like . . . like . . . I don't know! There are no words for it, but it was the worst night of my life!"

"It was not," I said. "You told me yourself that the worst night of your life was when you went to your cousin's wedding reception and got caught making out with his brother's girl-friend."

My mom choked a little on that one but tried to remain stoic.

"This surpassed that," he said.

"Aw, Rudy, you know this was fun. You'll tell our grand-children about it."

"I won't have to, because the whole town will tell them first.

It will be etched in gold. They will probably teach it in local history class."

"You're overreacting. Again, I might add." I began filling my mother in on the night's activities as Rudy paced the kitchen floor with the remnants of soufflé still on his face. He was about to tell his side of the story when my mother jumped in.

"All right," Mom said and held her hand up. "That's enough. No, the evening did not go as planned, but Torie was hardly to blame there, Rudy. She couldn't help that all those people were there and she couldn't help that Eleanore decided to steal the briefcase."

"Great. You're ganging up on me," he accused. "She could have gotten herself killed. Let's be serious."

"It's hard to be serious when you have soufflé on your face," Mom said and then tried not to laugh.

"I know I could have gotten hurt," I said. "But Eleanore was just way off tonight. I couldn't let her get killed."

"By the way," Mom said, "I think I figured out the code."

"What?" I asked.

"You know, the code."

"What are you talking about?"

"Evidently, Mary got into the papers on your desk. She drew me this really neat picture of a horse and a princess. It just happened to be on the back of the photocopy of that document with all of the numbers on it."

"And?"

"And, I think I've cracked it."

"I don't believe it," I said.

Mom pulled the piece of paper out from under a newspaper and showed me. "I assumed that the dashes were intended to differentiate between words. Then I took the two-letter words and figured that they were words like *it, my, to, is*. Then I tried the old Boy Scout trick of skipping every other letter. Which didn't work, but I assumed that this was the type of code that we were dealing with."

Even Rudy had come over and watched over her shoulder.

"All right," I said, "cut to the chase."

"Well the vowels are numbered first, but from the end of the alphabet. Y is a one, U is a two. And so on. Then if you skip the first letter from the end and number the consonants only you skip every other one, then go back and number the remaining consonants."

I sat down on that one.

"And this worked?" Rudy asked.

"Like a dream," Mom said. "Of course it has taken me two days and I've tried at least seven different combinations. This is what it says: 'Between thirty-five and forty lat, and ninety-five and ninety long, there is a castle erected anew, wherein lies the fortune of the Merovees obtained from the Pyrenees. Once in this castle anew with the river on your right, it sleeps beneath Queens own home waiting your arrival. Beware! Ill fortune awaits.' "

" 'Castle erected anew,' " Rudy said. "It must mean New Kassel."

"That's what I thought," Mom said.

" 'The fortune of the Merovees.' Tonight, in the briefcase," I said, "Eleanore and I saw some papers that talked about a group of people called the Merovee Knights. I wonder if they are referring to Merovingian when they say Merovee. Obtained from the Pyrenees would mean either Spain or France, most likely France."

"Yes," Mom said. "But what is 'Queens own home'?"

"I have no idea."

The phone rang and we all jumped.

"Hello? Sheriff Brooke," I said.

"Torie, I wanted to let you know that we picked up Yvonne Mezalaine tonight," he said.

"And?"

"She claims not to know Ransford Dooley. She said that she had been invited here by Marie to attend a meeting in St. Louis with some associates of Marie's. She said that they were Lanny Lockheart and Andrew Wheaton."

"What about being her sister? Is she still claiming to be Marie's half sister?"

"She said that she was not related to Marie, but that she knew her on a professional level for many years. But guess what?"

"What?"

"We found the stolen papers in her car."

NEW KASSEL GAZETTE

THE NEWS YOU MIGHT MISS
by Eleanore Murdoch

Tobias says thank you for his new accordion. The speed with which New Kassel residents gave donations for the accordion was amazing.

Right now we only have four apple dumpling recipes entered in our contest. One of those entries belongs to Jalena Keith. Come on, New Kassel residents. Jalena wins all of the recipe contests. At least give her some competition this year! You may drop off your entry at the Birk/Zeis home, Pierre's, or Torie's office at the Gaheimer House.

And a note to whoever was jogging in the nude on the bridge last Tuesday night: at least buy yourself some sneakers.

Until next time.

Eleanore

Twenty-two

I knocked on the door of room seven of the Murdoch Inn. I wanted some answers and I thought Andrew was the man to give them to me. I did not hear any noise from inside, but I stuck around and knocked again. I looked down at my feet, noticed the mud on my L.A. Gears, and knocked yet another time.

Up the steps came Andrew Wheaton, just the man I was trying to get to answer the door. He stiffened when he saw me, making his muscular neck seem out of proportion to the rest of his body. He'd gone for the *American Gigolo* look this morning. His pants, shirt, and tie were all different shades of olive and khaki green. His shoes, a shiny black, were spiffy and barely looked worn.

"Mrs. O'Shea," he said. "What a surprise."

"I doubt that," I said. "May I speak with you a moment? It's important."

He honestly looked like he was afraid of me. I am about as unimposing a person as one can find. I'm short. I dress casually. There isn't an anxious bone in my body. I'm also a woman. Not that I think women are unimposing, but a lot of men do.

"All right," he said. He unlocked the door and I followed him inside. The inside of his room was done in country blue with a hardwood floor and oak bed. He placed his keys next to the pitcher and bowl, resting on a dressing table.

"Well? What is it?"

He seemed unsure and nervous. He glanced around the room several times before finally looking at me.

"I want to know just what the heck is going on."

"What do you mean?"

"I know you saw Marie before she died. You were in her house. You could have killed her. Not that I think that you did. I'm not even sure that she was killed on purpose. I think it could have been an accident. But you had ample opportunity."

"Motive?" he asked.

"That's what I want to discuss. The motive here seems to be something so far-fetched that I can't conceive it. It seems that Marie was killed for some documents and letters that pertain to the French crown, the man in the iron mask, a treasure, hell, just throw in the kitchen sink. I know that you are some sort of Merovee Knight, whatever the heck that is. What is going on?"

He looked around the room, even more nervous than before. "I didn't kill her."

"Okay, who did?"

"I don't know," he answered. "I'm going to fill you in on a few things only because I believe it will only be a matter of time until you figure it out." He walked over to the window and looked out. "A long time ago there were the Crusades. You know, the war against the Muslims, the Christians trying to take over the Holy Land. There were the Knights Templar. You familiar with them?"

"Yes, vaguely."

"The Knights Templar were in charge of keeping the road to Jerusalem safe. They were also the keepers of a great treasure.

164

They believed that the true heir to the French throne was descended from the Merovingian kings that occupied the throne before Hugh Capet took over."

"All right. I follow you there."

"They hid the treasure in France. A priest by the name of Berenger Sauniere found this treasure and had it removed. Nobody knew where."

"Are the documents themselves the treasure?" I asked. "Are they that priceless?"

He sat down on the edge of his bed and ran his fingers through his hair. "No. Those documents were in a building in Nice, Italy. They tell unbelievable secrets that I'm not even going to discuss with you. They were the Templars' ammunition against Louis."

"And Henri de Lorraine?"

"He was the descendant that the Templars were trying to bring to power. The king wouldn't kill him, because the Templars would only replace him with another heir."

"Why wasn't something done in 1703 when the prisoner died?"

"There was no need to replace him," Andrew said. "The Order was in complete chaos and civil war. There was no longer a threat. The Order could not regroup."

"So, where do these Merovee Knights come in?"

"We are a division, a branch of the Templars. The Templars no longer exist," he stated.

Talk about paranoia. I began looking over my shoulder at every little noise. "I don't get it. How does Marie fit in? What was the treasure that this Sauniere guy had?"

"The treasure is more wealth than you can imagine. Gold. Jewels. Enough to start your own country with. Marie's father was a high officer in the Order. He was given the documents.

He had an operative here in the United States by the name of Gaston—"

"Levaldieu."

"Yes. Gaston was to find an inconspicuous out-of-the-way place for the treasure. Which he did. He wired back to Mr. Jaillard the locations in a coded message."

"So, Jaillard sent the treasure?"

"Yes. It's here, somewhere in New Kassel. It was originally to be given to the correct heir. When that happened they were to take over France or create their own country, by force if they had to. But they had no idea Hitler would come along and awaken powerful countries like the United States. The thought of an heir of the Merovingian line taking over the world is now ludicrous."

"How did Marie fit in?" I asked again.

"Marie was a member of the Merovee Knights, but she never let on like she knew the whereabouts of the treasure and she never, ever let on like she had the documents. They were supposedly hidden and her father never revealed the hiding place."

"So, she figured out the coded message and knew to come here."

"Yes. Lanny began thinking that she had the documents about five years ago, because of something she said. He was absolutely convinced."

"So did everybody and their uncle follow her here or were you all invited?" I asked.

"We were coming to St. Louis for the meeting. She wrote and told everybody that this is where she was living, but never let on like this was the place of the treasure. Lanny just knew that the treasure must be close by."

"Did he kill her?"

"I don't know, Mrs. O'Shea," he said. "Now please go. I've told you more than enough. And more than I had to."

"So this was all just a big treasure hunt?"

"For millions, Mrs. O'Shea."

"How do you know all of this is true? How do you know that you and the Merovee Knights and the Templars have not been taken for a wild ride? A practical joke. I've read some on the Templars and I know that it is said that King Philip in the 1300s stripped them of their land and their money. They were tried as heretics. I think you've been taken."

"I don't expect you to believe me," he said. "But the treasure was sent here for safekeeping for the true heir. It was not meant to go to private individuals. It was not meant for greedy treasure hunters. Somewhere along the line, the Merovee Knights have forgotten that we are to protect the bloodline."

"How does Yvonne fit in?" I asked. I didn't want him to get too carried away with the hidden agenda of the Knights. I didn't want to witness any secret handshake and all that.

"She is a member as well."

"Well, I think she just may be Marie's murderer," I said. I turned to leave, got my hand on the door, and stopped. "Have you ever heard of Ransford Dooley?" I asked.

It had occurred to me that Ransford might have access to some of his real grandfather's papers. Maybe he figured out what was going on. Maybe he and Marie were in cahoots together to get the treasure. Then decided to take it all for himself. Or Marie decided not to share it.

Treasure. That was pure nonsense. There was no real treasure. That sort of thing was fairy-tale garbage. I didn't really believe that Henri de Lorraine was the man in the iron mask, either.

Andrew shook his head in the negative. He did not know Ransford Dooley.

"Well, at your next meeting," I began, "you can tell everybody to hang it up, because Yvonne was found with the documents in her car. The documents are now evidence in a murder investigation. Nobody will ever see them again."

He didn't look too happy with me when I told him that. As a matter of fact he looked like he'd swallowed a bug. I turned and opened the door.

"By the way, I don't believe *your* motives in this are innocent, either. If you truly believed that the treasure was to be held for the true heir, you wouldn't have your sticky fingers in the middle of it. You're just as greedy as all the rest, so don't play the honorable knight with me."

Twenty-three

It was nearly midnight and we were engaged in a moonlit hayride. The silver light from the full moon cast a celestial glow on all of us in the wagon. Rudy sat next to me, the girls in front of us at our feet. They don't normally stay up this late, but the midnight hayrides that go with the Octoberfest were one of the year's few exceptions.

Sheriff Brooke was in the process of loading my mother on board. He reached down and put one hand under her legs and the other behind her back and she wrapped her arms around his neck. He sat her on a lump of hay and then folded her chair and set it aside. Then he climbed up with us.

My father would lift my mother whenever we would go places, too. He did that when we went to the Grand Canyon. My mother nearly died of vertigo. It was not a fun vacation.

My father would carry her even now, if they were still married. But I had to be honest, I couldn't imagine my father ever going on a hayride. At midnight, no less.

Mary yawned and leaned her head back on Rudy's leg.

"Ready?" Elmer asked.

"Yes," I said.

Elmer gave the reins of the horse a snap and we were off. We went through town at a fantastically slow pace, listening to the horses' shoes clop on the blacktop. The midnight hayrides were something that the town did for tourists during the Octoberfest. It was three dollars a wagonload.

"It's your turn tomorrow night, Rudy," Elmer said over his shoulder.

"I know," he said.

"Daddy?" asked Rachel. "Are you driving the wagon tomorrow night?"

"One of them."

"Can I go with you?"

"Sure," he said.

Sheriff Brooke leaned forward. "Torie, what're your thoughts on Yvonne?"

"Don't know."

"Do you really believe all of that garbage about the Knights Templar and a treasure?" he asked.

"Everything that Andrew said was based in truth. There were Knights Templars. There was a man in the iron mask. Henri de Lorraine was the heir to Charles. There was a priest named Sauniere that found something at a church in Rennes-le-Château. Many think it was a treasure. Marie's family is connected to all of it. I believe all of it. I just don't believe that it could happen in New Kassel."

"Why not?"

"I don't know. I guess if it were true, then the safe little town that I know and love will seem—I don't know—tainted."

"Could you guys stop talking shop?" Rudy asked.

"Is there anything to link Yvonne to Marie's house? Like fibers?" I asked.

"There is no physical evidence," he said.

We were silent as Elmer turned down the street that would

take us through the park in town. The chill bit at my face and made me shiver.

"I'm glad we all wore flannel," Mom said.

The girls climbed up on the hay next to Rudy and me, and watched the street ahead of them. The harvest moon was so brilliant, it was as if we were riding under streetlights. I saw the smile on Mary's face and the anticipation in Rachel's eyes. The smell of wood burning filled the night air, making me forget about summer and anticipate the coming winter—which, once it got here, I'd say that I couldn't believe I'd ever wished for.

"What about Dooley?" I asked.

"Tons of physical evidence," Sheriff Brooke said. "But you'd expect to find hairs and fibers from him. He was a friend of hers and visited often. He also claims that he is the grandson of Hermann Gaheimer and that he never heard of anyone named Levaldieu."

"Either Elizabeth Gaheimer never told her children the truth or Dooley's lying."

"Can't prove it."

"Can't prove much of anything in this case," I mumbled.

I turned with Rachel to see just where the horse was headed. The smell of hay was starting to irritate my sinuses, but what didn't? I was going to have to see an allergist soon.

"Ooo," Mary said and pointed to the horse. "That horse is poopin'."

Rachel laughed. Rudy tried hard not to. Mother covered her eyes with her hand and shook her head. Children are so honest. Not just honest. No-holds-barred-I'm-telling-you-exactly-what-I-think type of honesty.

"That's nice, Mary. Try to use a different word next time."

"The one Grandpa uses?" Rachel asked.

"No! I mean, no, dear. Not the one Grandpa uses."

I looked at Rudy and he was smiling. "Don't look at me," he said. "My dad never says things like that."

We passed by the Santa Lucia Church, the graveyard looking particularly festive. It was October and somehow graveyards just take on a different look. I thought about Marie. I was sorry that she had died. I was sorry anytime anybody died. But I couldn't help but feel anger. I was angry that a person's greed could lead them down the wrong paths. Suffice it to say, if it weren't for the promise of millions, Marie would be alive. Whether or not the treasure was real, the Merovee Knights believed it was real. It got her killed, and it nearly got Camille killed.

"What if the person that killed Marie is none of the above suspects? What if it's not Yvonne, Dooley, Lanny, or Andrew? What if it's somebody we haven't seen yet?"

"Would you please stop talking about this stuff?" Rudy asked again. "Just for one night."

I saw the rectory and remembered that there were a few names of people on the register that we had not found yet. Could it be one of them? I thought about the fact that Sister Lucy was in possession of the registry, and it reminded me that Sister Lucy was one of the few friends that Marie had in town. I wondered if maybe she could tell me something. Like friends of Marie's that we didn't know about.

"Did you know," Rudy began, "that the Santa Lucia Church is named after Saint Lucy?"

"Who is Saint Lucy?" Rachel asked.

"She loved God very much and was proud of her virtue."

"What's verr chew?" Rachel asked carefully.

"Her . . . innocence," he said. "Anyway, this man came along and completely fell in love with her. He said that one look into her eyes, made him want to . . . want to . . . be with her for the rest of his life. His passion consumed him and he couldn't contain himself."

"What happened?" Rachel asked.

"She gouged her eyes out and served them to him on a silver platter."

"Rudy!"

"Ooo, Dad," Rachel said.

"All for the love of God and in the name of virtue."

"I think I'd rather not have verr chew," Rachel said.

Out of the mouths of babes.

Twenty-four

Sister Lucy sat perfectly poised in her black habit. A silver crucifix hung around her neck, and she played with the plain gold band she wore that represented her marriage to Christ. I'd seen her a few times without her habit and knew that she had reddish hair. Eyebrows and eyelashes the same shade as her hair added the only color on her makeup-free face. She had dark brown eyes and an overly large bottom lip.

"It was good of you to see me," I said to her.

"That's all right," she answered. She was in her mid-forties, maybe older, but she had the vibrance of youth.

"It just occurred to me that your name, Lucy, is the same as the church. Santa Lucia."

"Yes. But I had this name long before I'd ever heard of Santa Lucia Church."

"I was wondering if I could see the register from Marie's funeral again. I hate to bother you with something like that, but it's terribly important."

"Certainly," she said.

She got up and walked to a plain desk situated in the corner. There wasn't much in the room. A crucifix on the wall, one on a shelf, and a dresser. Her bed had no headboard but was graced with a blue and white checked quilt. There were a few photos on the dresser with a pink scarf. The photo on her desk was in a silver frame and was of three small children.

She reached in the top drawer and pulled out the register. She handed it to me and sat down.

"I don't see any names in here other than the ones I saw the first time," I said, and so turned to the rest of those names. "Tell me, Sister, do you know who Paul Garland is?"

"He used to be a priest."

"Used to be?"

"Yes. He fell in love with the night-cleaning lady at his church and got married. I think Marie knew him from the town she lived in before this."

"Where was that?"

"I think Chicago."

"And Sally Reuben? Who is she?"

"A student. Back from Marie's teaching days."

"I wonder how they knew that she died?" I asked.

Sister Lucy said nothing.

"How long did you know her?" I asked.

"Just since she moved here. About two years," she answered.

"When did you see her last?"

"The Monday before she died. We drove into Wisteria to buy her some shoes. Said she couldn't buy a decent pair of shoes in New Kassel."

"I don't suppose that you have any idea who would have reason to kill her, do you?" I asked.

"Do you really think that she was murdered?"

"I don't think she fell down the steps because she miscalculated the step, no. After what happened with my friend I'm beginning to think that it could have been an accident. The result of an argument. A court would be hard-pressed to prove that it was premeditated," I said.

"I have no idea," she said after a moment's hesitation.

"Well, if you think of somebody or something you can give Sheriff Brooke a call," I said.

"I certainly will," she said.

"I'm going to go now."

I got up and headed for the door. "Oh, would you do me a huge favor?" I asked.

"What?"

"My grandmother, my dad's mom, she was Catholic and I was wondering if you would . . ."

"Say a prayer for her?"

"Please? And light a candle?"

"You know, you could do it yourself," she said.

"I know. But somehow I get the impression that God listens to you guys more than me."

"That is positively not true," she said. "If he hears a new voice speaking to him, it may perk him up."

I wondered how she envisioned God when he was perked up. As my dad always says, "Two hundred and fifty million people, that's two hundred and fifty million interpretations of God." I agreed with that, because I couldn't imagine God perked up and Sister Lucy could. It's great to live in a free country.

"Well, just to be on the safe side?" I said.

"I will light a candle for your grandmother."

"Thank you."

Twenty-five

I don't believe it," I said. "Eleanore printed a retraction on the article that she wrote about Sylvia being responsible for the death of Sophie Gaheimer."

My mother put down her fork and looked quite pleased. We were eating breakfast, and I had stalled long enough. I didn't want to go to the Gaheimer House and work because I had the feeling that I would run into Sylvia. Since she had given me Hermann's diary, I had scarcely seen her. We passed each other when I did the tours, but she was usually gone by the time I finished.

I'm not complaining, mind you. I had been trying to figure out how I was going to tell her that she wasn't responsible for Sophie's death without informing her that Hermann let the culprit go unchecked.

"I suppose you shook her up the other night," Mom said.

I swirled my pancakes in the syrup and took a bite. "Yeah, and she even printed that it was her mistake, that she had copied the wrong information."

"Goodness," Mom said. "A trace of humanity."

"Yeah. Wonder what she wants," I said.

Fritz was seated next to my chair waiting for any scraps that might fall his way. I deliberately dropped a piece of bacon.

"Bacon isn't good for dogs," Mom said.

"It's not good for people either, but we still eat it."

"Nobody has claimed him," she said. "Are you going to keep him?"

I looked down at his brown eyes and he cocked his head sideways. He knew when he was onstage. He knew that how adorable he looked at that moment could make his future. He gave a soft little bark, as if to say, You know you love me.

"It has been over a week," I said. "Yes, I suppose I will."

My mother gave a little huff, but it was forced. She had grown to like Fritz as much as we had. "You like him," I said.

"I tolerate him," she corrected.

"Yeah. Whatever." I knew better. And what's more, she knew that I knew better. "I'm going to have to tell Eleanore how much I appreciate this. Even though I don't want to."

"You better get to work," Mom said.

•

I could not find Sylvia Pershing when I first entered the Gaheimer House. I walked through the foyer, the ballroom, my office, the kitchen. No Sylvia. Finally, I got a hunch as to where she would be. I walked up the stairs, the familiar creak of the ninth step going virtually unnoticed. I ran my finger along the oak banister, trying hard to imagine life in this house at the turn of the century.

"Sylvia?"

It was a loveless home. A man with three children that were not his own, his wife playing him for a fool. A man immersing himself into his work, this town. He was all but dead inside, and then a breath of fresh air entered his life. Sylvia Pershing.

I have to admit, it was hard for me to imagine Sylvia as a

breath of anything, except maybe a dragon. Hermann had seen her differently. Probably because she *was* different then. She'd been young and beautiful, and in love with a man that she could not have. Not in the legal sense anyway. I say that because I think Hermann was hers in every other sense. Mind, body, and soul. And what a man he must have been. I'd often thought of him as the Ernest Hemingway type in the recent months since I'd discovered what had transpired between him and Sylvia. She was but a girl. He was close to eighty.

I turned left when I reached the upstairs, following the mauve Victorian floor runner. At the end of the hall was Hermann's den. This room represented Hermann in every way. An oval photograph of him hung above the large mahogany desk. His pipe holder sat on the left-hand shelf, with his four or five pipes still resting in it.

And there sat Sylvia Pershing: quiet, submersed, withdrawn.

"Sylvia?"

"Yes," she said, without turning.

"It's me, Torie."

"I'm well aware of who you are. And your name is Victory. I can never understand why you butcher that name. Don't you know what it means?" she asked.

Her back was to me. Ancient, gnarled fingers played with the tobacco tin that sat next to the pipe holder on the desk, as if she gleaned some comfort from touching things that he once used.

"Yes, Sylvia. I'm aware of what my name means." My name has a dual meaning. I was named after a ghost, a ghost that haunted an old mill, down in Pine Branch. Victory LeBreau was her name. But my mother also named me Victory because I was a victory. She was told that she could never have children.

And was informed by several cruel family members that even if she could have children, no normal man would want a cripple in that way. She proved them wrong. I was her Victory.

"Sylvia, I've come to return Hermann's diary," I said.

Her hand stopped its loving caress of the tobacco tin for a split second. She resumed as abruptly as she had stopped.

"I told you to keep it."

"I've read it," I said. I waited for her to say something. I would welcome her hateful prattle right about now. "I think you should have it back."

I wanted to walk around and face her, but didn't know if I should. This was Sylvia's territory. She was my elder, not to mention my boss. Finally, I could stand it no more and walked around her chair and looked down at her. Her gray eyes did not look at me. They seemed to look straight through my stomach and out the window behind me. The braids that wound around her head looked loose and unkempt. She was tired. No, she was depressed.

I handed the diary out to her. "Sylvia. I've read it. He did not blame you for Sophie's death. She did not commit suicide. She knew about you, and she didn't care. She had her own lover and had been with him for years. None of her children were Hermann's and he knew it."

Sylvia looked up at me as this new knowledge registered with her.

"That's right," I said as I knelt down in front of her chair. "Hermann could not have children."

Her age-spotted hand went to her mouth, and tears welled in her eyes. They threatened to spill forth, but she kept them in check.

"He loved you more than life itself. Please read it. Find out in his voice just what you meant to him," I said and pressed the diary into her open hand. "I'll take it back someday," I said. "But this belongs to you until you depart this world."

The tears finally spilled, leaving one long streak down each cheek. Then she sobbed. I leaned forward and hugged her, not knowing if I should. I tried to pull away, but Sylvia held me close. Finally, the shame, the fear, the doubt of seventy-five years came out with a force. She had faced her demon, the demon that raised its ugly head all of her life. It was out. And it wasn't so scary after all.

Twenty-six

I sat at the kitchen table looking through some papers for the history of New Kassel that I was working on. My mother sat quietly at the other end of the table, crocheting or knitting, I always get the two confused. Suddenly I saw something on one of the pages. Laughter rolled out of me uncontrollably. I took a drink of Dr Pepper and, as a result of the laughter, it snarfed out my nose. My mother looked appropriately appalled at my table manners because, after all, she was the person who had taught them to me. One can never get it through one's parents' heads that we children learned everything correctly. We just choose to ignore it sometimes. But this incident was an accident. I wasn't snarfing my soda because of bad manners. I snarfed my soda because of hysterical laughter.

"Would you mind telling me what is so funny?" Mother asked.

I would if I could get it out. I got up and walked into the living room, holding my stomach from my unexpected outburst of laughter. I sat down on my piano bench in the living room, sending whatever sheet music was sitting there onto the floor.

"Hee hee hee, whoo, whoo whoo."

My mother followed me into the living room. "Have you suddenly lost your marbles?"

"Yes," I managed. I slapped my knee. My side hurt and my nostrils seemed to have a life of their own.

"There is nothing more irritating than another person laughing hysterically when you have no idea what they are laughing about!"

"I'm sorry, I'm sorry," I said. "Just let me breathe."

She crossed her arms and raised an eyebrow. She would have tapped her foot if she could have.

"Okay," I said. "I think I'm all right now. Guess what I discovered?"

"What?"

"The treasure . . . 'Queens own home,' " I said. "Remember we couldn't figure out what 'Queens own home' meant in the riddle that you decoded?"

"Yes?"

"In 1922, Alexander and Alma Queen . . . get it? Queen . . . Alexander Queen lived at number 4 River Point Road."

I love watching the dawn of realization when it hits people.

"Number 4 River Point Road is now the location of the Murdoch Inn," I said. "The treasure is hidden under the Murdoch Inn! If only Eleanore knew!" I said. Laughter bubbled again and I soon found myself in a worse state of fits than before. "And you wanna know what's worse?" I asked. "Andrew Wheaton and Lanny Lockheart have been staying there all of this time! The treasure was right under their butts the whole time. Hee hee hee. Life is good."

My mother failed to catch the humor in this at first. Then the thought of it sort of grew on her, and soon she was laughing as hard as I was.

"It must be in a trunk or something, because that's what the key must be for."

"What key?" she asked as she wiped her eyes.

"The key that I found with . . . the . . . documents . . . Hey, you know what? I just thought. I need to head over to Santa Lucia."

"Victory! What key? Are you saying that you have a key that you didn't tell anybody about?"

"Well, if nobody knew about it, then it wasn't any threat, now was it?"

"Oy vey," she said. We're not Jewish, but that has been a favorite phrase of hers since I was a child.

"Gotta go, Mom. I'll be home in time to fix dinner."

When in hot water, get out of the kettle.

I pulled into the driveway of Santa Lucia and parked by the rectory about three minutes later. Something had bugged me the other day when I visited Sister Lucy. When I asked her how Marie's friends from out of town had learned of her death, Sister said nothing. She did not say she did not know. She just didn't say anything. I didn't know what it meant, but it bugged me.

Sister Margaret Elizabeth led me to Sister Lucy's room. "Wait here," she said. "She'll just be a second."

"Thank you," I said to the very young nun. She looked about twenty-two.

I promised myself that I would not snoop around in this nun's room. Even I have my limits. It killed me, but I still had my limits. I didn't see anything wrong with just walking around and looking at what was out, though.

The photograph on the desk was horizontal, and of three little girls in what looked like their slips standing waist deep in a creek or lake. They had their arms around each other, smiling as only the young can smile. The smile said, "We are immortal, we will never change, never grow old." We all have the luxury of unconsciously believing that at some point in our lives.

"Mrs. O'Shea," Sister Lucy said from behind me. I jumped as if I were doing something wrong, and for once I wasn't.

"Oh, hello," I said. "You scared the daylights out of me."

"What can I do for you?"

"Well, I don't know, actually. I was wondering, the other day when I asked you how Marie's friends had been notified of her death, you didn't answer."

"She had several friends in town. They were all going to a business meeting or something like it. Plus there was Mr. Dooley. Maybe one of those individuals called her other friends," she said.

"Why didn't anybody call any of her family? I'm sure she had cousins and such," I said as I watched her face grow from tolerant to impatient. "I mean, I know she had two sisters."

"I wouldn't know," the nun said.

But she would know. She was her friend. A very close friend. I glanced over at the photograph on her desk. "Who are they?" I asked.

"What? What does that photograph have to do with anything?"

"Who are the girls in the photo?"

"Me and some childhood friends," she said. "I don't see what it matters."

I hate it when my brain decides to clear a passage that I can suddenly see through, after it's been foggy. I feel stupid when that happens. She seemed unnaturally nervous over the photograph, which only added to my epiphany. Well, that and the fact that in the distance of the photograph was a castle. How many castles are there in America?

185

"You're lying," I said to her. "That is you and Marie and—tell me if I'm wrong—Yvonne? Marie was your sister, wasn't she?"

Sister Lucy, aside from swallowing heavily, showed no outward appearance that I was right or wrong. But the swallow told me enough. I was right, or I was damned close.

"I think you should leave, Mrs. O'Shea. I am going to report your behavior to Father Bingham," she said.

"Fine. You do that," I said. "Tell me, Sister, why the secrecy? So Marie was your sister, big deal. Or is this some more of that cloak-and-dagger garbage? You know, the Merovee Knights and all that?"

"Get out," she said.

I walked to the door, taking a quick inventory of everything in the room, hoping that I would see something, anything, that could connect Marie to Sister Lucy. "It would make sense," I said. "Marie didn't let in a stranger the night she was killed, and she didn't let in a man. She let in a woman. That would more likely be the case," I said.

"I don't know what you're talking about," Sister Lucy said. "And if you continue to sling accusations my way, you had better have an awfully good attorney backing you up."

"I wasn't accusing. I simply said that it would make sense that a woman living alone would not let in a man at that time of the night, but that she would let in a woman. A woman she trusted. Her sister," I said. "That's all. I didn't say it was you. I didn't even say that I believed that's what happened. I just said it would make sense."

"I think you should go now," Sister Lucy said.

I looked around the room, but aside from the photograph, everything was religious in nature. Paintings of Christ and the Virgin, the wood and ivory crucifix, a print of the Angel

Gabriel. There was nothing else to learn here, unless Sister Lucy decided to spill her guts, which I didn't expect anytime soon.

"Forgive me, Sister, if I'm wrong," I said. "But if I'm right?"

"I suspect that you suffer from an overactive imagination. One that is given to great supposition," she declared.

"Whatever you say, Dorothee. That is you, right? You would be Dorothee L. Jaillard. Let me guess, the 'L' stands for Lucy? Or Lucia?" I asked.

"Get out!" she said, quite angrily.

Anger is the quickest way to know when you're right, or at least hitting a nerve. My husband gets more angry at me when I'm right than when I'm wrong.

"You know the records will be easy enough to check," I said.

She said nothing to that. It was clear that I had her.

"Good day, Sister."

Twenty-seven

Just outside of Fraulein Krista's Speisehaus, Tobias Thorley
stood in his blue and gold knicker outfit playing the accordion. I winked at him as I walked by, and he winked back.

It was gorgeous in New Kassel. Once the calendar turns to
October, Missouri comes alive. Brilliant blue skies so full of
oxygen that you nearly get woozy just breathing it, and splashes
of red and gold along the countryside are Nature's way of saying thank you. It says thank you for putting up with three feet
of snow in March, seventy-degree weather in January, sixteen
below on Easter Sunday, and one-hundred-ten-degree weather
for the entire month of August. Missouri's weather is just that
unpredictable, and October seems to be the only month that
can be predicted with any accuracy.

The aroma of apple turnovers wafted by my particularly delicate nose as I crossed the street. Halfway across, the aroma
turned to bratwurst. The combination is indescribable.

Tourists milled the street with their mouths full, stomachs
fuller, and eyes the size of saucers. Children with brightly
colored balloons tied to their wrists looked ready to fall over
from exhaustion as the parents kept dragging them from shop to
shop.

"Look, there's the lady who gave the tour yesterday," I heard one child say as he pointed to me. I waved back from the sidewalk in front of the Gaheimer House.

I entered the house to find Sheriff Brooke waiting in the parlor. He was in uniform, with his hat in one hand.

"Glad you could make it," I said. "Where's Sylvia and Wilma?"

"Wilma's turning bratwurst over at the Smells Good, and Sylvia is helping Helen out at the candy shop."

"Good, don't let me forget to lock up then," I said.

"Where are we going?" he asked.

"I'll tell you when we get in the car. Did you bring your squad car or your yellow junker?" I asked.

"The squad car," he said.

"I guess it will have to do," I said. I left him standing in the parlor as I went to get Marie's file from my office. "All right, let's go."

I wore my bright orange sweatshirt with the white ghosts and black cats on it. Black pants and my black Reeboks completed the outfit. We walked down the street about a block and passed by a private residence that already had Halloween decorations out. A large scarecrow was perched on the banister of the porch, at least eight pumpkins sat all around, and a real live black cat sat swaying its tail back and forth.

We got in his car and neither one of us said a word until we were on I-55.

"Okay, what's up?" he asked.

"I know who killed Marie," I said.

He said nothing. He waited for my explanation with the patience of Job.

"I went back to see Sister Lucy," I said. "And I noticed a photograph of these three little girls and I remembered that

Marie had two sisters. It seemed to fit. Sure enough, Sister Lucy is really Dorothee Lucia Jaillard."

"But she doesn't have an accent."

"Well, they left France in like 1950; she was only four or five. Marie had no accent either. Anyway, remember how Yvonne had said that she was Marie's sister?"

"Yes."

"Well, when I said something about not recognizing the name Yvonne as being on Marie's records, she said that she was her half sister."

"Why do that if you're her whole sister? Is that what you're getting at? That Yvonne is Marie's whole sister?"

"What I'm getting at is Yvonne was using a fake name. So to cover her tracks that she was using a fake name so that we wouldn't get suspicious of her, she made up the story about being Marie's half sister."

"And? She killed her?" Sheriff Brooke asked. "We already know that she has the documents, that she tried to kill Camille. She denies that of course. Is that what you're getting at?"

"No, no, no. See, that's the tricky part. I have no bloody idea who Yvonne is. Camille is Marie's other sister."

"What?"

"That's right. See?" I said as I pointed to the charts. "She's listed as Jeanne C. Jaillard born in 1938. I called my cousin in Virginia and he called another cousin. It gets confusing. Suffice it to say, Camille Lombarde's birth record states that she was born Jeanne Camille Jaillard in Besançon, France. She married somebody named Lombarde."

Sheriff Brooke said nothing.

"Well?"

"I'm thinking," he said. "So, you're suggesting that Camille killed Marie."

"Yes. Remember how the car in her garage still had gas in it? We assumed it died."

"Camille staged the whole thing so that you'd think that the documents were stolen. She turned off the engine herself," he said.

"Yup."

"How did you ever think that Camille was the other sister?" he asked.

"I didn't at first. It was only when you told me that there was no record of an Yvonne Mezalaine that I knew something was up. I thought she'd have legally changed her name or something from Jeanne C. Jaillard. Then I saw a crucifix in Sister Lucy's room. It was cherry wood with ivory. Camille had one that was identical. Then the inconsistencies in Camille's story took on new meaning."

Sheriff Brooke put on his blinker and turned. "You realize what this means, don't you?"

"What?"

"Yvonne was caught with the documents. She and Camille must be working together."

"There's a possibility that you can never make a case out of this. If you can't prove that she or Yvonne were at Marie's house, you have no case. And you'll probably never get a pre-meditation conviction. Their lawyers would say that it was an accident, and there is nothing you can do to prove otherwise," I said.

When we finally pulled on to Camille street, my heart was pumping and face splotchy. I was wired.

"I think that you should let me go in and speak with her alone," I said.

"No."

"She's not going to say anything while you're in there," I

said. "She won't say a word without a lawyer. But I think she would talk to me. Then you can use me as a witness."

"That's entrapment."

"How can it be? There's no recording device. If you just show up on your own accord after five minutes, it will be just like she and I were carrying on a private conversation. As long as I don't record anything and you're not eavesdropping, how can it be entrapment?"

He parked the car with that stonewall look that he gets.

"Fine. Don't use me as a witness. I'll never tell you anything that she says, but I've got to know."

He still said nothing.

"Dammit, Colin! She used me. I thought she was my friend. Now I have to know what happened. For my own personal sanity," I pleaded.

"All right," he said. "You've got five minutes. That's all you're getting. No more, no less. I'm calling in the St. Louis police."

"Okay," I said and got out of his car. I walked the half a block down the street, walked up her steps, and rang the doorbell.

She did not look surprised to see me. Sister Lucy had probably called and told her that I was coming.

"Torie," she said. "Come in."

"I can't stay long," I said to her. "I've just come to tell you that I know everything. I know the complete truth to the whole damn scheme."

"You only think you know."

Great, she didn't deny it. She was going to play fair.

"I know that you are Jeanne Camille Jaillard, I know that you are Marie's sister."

"I don't deny these things."

"You killed her. And you had Yvonne run me off the road, didn't you?"

"No. I don't know what you're talking about. I haven't seen my sister in a long time."

I spoke too soon. She wasn't going to play fair.

"I'm sure that's what you're going to say," I said, "because the authorities will be hard-pressed to prove otherwise. And since nobody saw you at Marie's house, there's nothing anybody can do."

"Look, Torie. I didn't kill my sister," she said. She reached for an oak box with intricate carvings. She pulled out a cigarette and lit it with the lighter on the table. Funny, I never noticed that she smoked. "You can't imagine what I've been going through. Marie was a bitch, to put it bluntly. Oh, she was nice on the outside, never stepped on the cracks in the sidewalks, never killed spiders in her house. She was charitable, friendly, flirtatious. But she was greedy. She wanted the treasure all to herself. It was Father's."

"What do you mean?" I asked, unsure of where this was going.

"My father was the heir! It was his treasure. He sent it to this country, by way of a contact. The contact was unaware of who Father was. He was only doing what the Order told him to do: to set up a safe place for the treasure to be hidden, because there was dissension in the ranks, and World War I had shaken up everybody in Europe. Suddenly Europe wasn't a safe place. It was a good thing that Father sent the money out of the country, because during World War II, Hitler would have most assuredly found it."

"I don't understand."

"The man wired the location of the treasure in code to Father to pass on to the Grand Master. But the American contact disappeared. We came to this country to get the treasure, but for some reason Father could not find it. He hid the documents and he died in 1951. We told the Grand Master that we could not find Father's paperwork, but we had it all along. It was ours. But in this completely hypocritical world, my sisters and I were to be excluded from his inheritance."

"Why?"

"We were not men. My father had no sons. So, Marie and Lucy and myself decided that the treasure should be ours anyway and we would split it. Only Marie got way too greedy. She began following up leads and clues without telling us. She married the Grand Master of the Knights, hoping to get more information. She became obsessed with this treasure."

"What about your car? Why did it have gas in it?"

"It stalled. It really stalled," she said. "I didn't stage that. I don't know who did that to me. Oh, Torie, I can imagine how betrayed you must feel."

"You have no idea."

Her eyes filled with tears, one sneaking out the corner. "I couldn't believe my luck when you came to me with those documents. I knew that Marie had been living in New Kassel, but she never mentioned you. Lucy mentioned you once or twice, but not with any importance. When you showed up on my doorstep with those documents . . . well, I thought God was telling me to take my inheritance."

Sheriff Brooke knocked on the door, quite aggressively, sending Camille and I into nervous jumps.

"I have an alibi, Torie. The night Marie was killed, I was at a party," she said. "Four doors down at the Winchesters'. I was there until two in the morning, and then Sam Greenly walked me home and stayed the night."

I didn't know what to do. The fibers of my carefully constructed hypothesis just unraveled.

Sheriff Brooke knocked again.

"I have to get that," I said. "It's Sheriff Brooke." I went to the door and let him in. He looked around, expectantly.

"I think I was mistaken," I said to the sheriff.

•

"You think you were mistaken?" Sheriff Brooke screamed.

"I was so sure," I said to the dash in his car. "And I was right about her being Marie's sister."

"That's not exactly a crime, ya know," he said.

"One thing is for sure, it would certainly clear up one puzzling aspect," I said.

"What's that?"

"If Camille did not kill Marie, it would explain why Marie's grave was ransacked. If Camille had done it, there would be no reason to ransack her grave, because she already had the documents," I said.

"So it had to be somebody who was looking for the documents," he said.

"Exactly."

"Like who?" he asked.

"Well, that would leave Lanny Lockheart, Andrew Wheaton, Yvonne Mezalaine, Ransford Dooley, and possibly Sister Lucy."

"The nun?" he asked. "The nun didn't do it."

"Why are you so sure? Nuns sin, too, ya know."

"It gives me the willies just thinking about it. The nun," he said.

"Well, it probably wasn't her," I said. "She would probably have known about the documents from Camille."

"We're back to square one," he said.

"Not necessarily," I said. "I have a plan."

Twenty-eight

Eleanore," I said and smiled.

"What do you want, Torie? I am a busy woman," she answered from behind the counter.

"First of all, I'd like to thank you for the retraction you printed in your column," I said. She didn't verbally acknowledge what I said, but she nodded her head. "Secondly, Rudy told me that you wanted to see me."

"Oh, yes. I forgot. I've been meaning to tell you and the sheriff this and keep forgetting," she said. Patrons were milling about on the bottom floor of the Murdoch Inn, and Eleanore seemed suddenly careful. She looked from side to side before she finally told me what she wanted to say.

"What is it?"

"The night that Marie was killed, I remember that Mr. Lockheart came back to the inn very late."

"How late?"

"After midnight. I had totally forgotten about it. I assumed that he was just out, you know, somewhere," she said and waved her hand into the air. "I didn't even realize that this was the same night that Marie died until about two days ago and I remembered. Anyway, he seemed a little nervous, but not terribly so."

"Did he have anything with him? Was he carrying anything?"

"No."

"I have an idea. I ran it by the sheriff. He liked it," I said. "Now with this new information that you've given me, I think it's imperative that we try it. I'm just afraid that there is no way to prove who killed Marie unless we force the killer to tip his own hand. Would you like to help me?"

"What does it entail?" she asked.

Which means "yes" for Eleanore.

"When Mr. Lockheart and Mr. Wheaton come down for dinner or to check out, whatever it is their plans are, I want you to tell them, in a casual way of course—"

"Of course," she said. Her eyes were dancing around in her head in complete euphoria. She was going to get to help!

"—that I found irrevocable proof of who killed Marie Dijon and that I hid it on my aunt's farm in the cornfield. Make out like I'm going to use this as leverage to get the treasure. Or that I'm going to try and get the treasure for myself after I turn in the proof of who the killer is. Something along those lines. You can think up something."

"Treasure?" she asked.

"Just say it," I said. "Then as casually as you can, mention that I am working tonight at the Gaheimer House. It must appear natural, Eleanore, or they won't bite. It also wouldn't hurt to go by and see Joe at the bakery and tell him the same story when Mr. Dooley is within hearing range."

"You're going to try and catch her killer? You're going to trap them?" she asked anxiously. I had to keep myself from saying, "Down, girl, down."

"The sheriff and I are going to try. It may not work and

then we'll have to try something else, but we've got to try this."

"You can count on me," Eleanore said. Her rings made a rapping sound on the counter when she pounded her fist on it. "I will not fail you."

"Good," I said. "Get talking."

Twenty-nine

Eleanore was good for something. Spreading gossip.

Sheriff Brooke and I had recruited my Aunt Emily's help in this escapade. She and my uncle left the farm for a couple of days, after giving us permission to use her corn-field. I waited in her upstairs bedroom, overlooking the field. Waiting.

It was an old trick, but we were hoping it would work. After everything else that I had learned or figured out where this case was concerned, we banked on the killer not being able to take a chance that I hadn't found undeniable proof of who it was.

We spread it around that I would be working all evening and the sheriff even made it look good by staying in New Kassel until I called and told him that somebody was in the cornfield. He had left Deputy Miller with me. He was in the basement watching out the windows. I was in the house with the lights off, so nobody would suspect that I was upstairs guarding the cornfield.

Guardian of the Cornfield. Sounded like something out of a Stephen King novel. I liked it.

The hours ticked by. No, they crawled by. I couldn't read once the sun started to go down, because I couldn't have a light on in the house. Even my itty-bitty book light would have showed too much light had I used it. I had to sit in the dark.

I came back from the potty, two doors down on the left, and stumped my foot on the dresser just inside the door. The sky was still lit, but the sun was nearly gone. It was behind a ridge, so that I couldn't actually see it, but the light it gave off was evident.

Then I saw it. A dark figure walked into the corn and nearly disappeared. I could see him emerge every now and then as he went methodically up and down every row in the cornfield. He'd be here all night, checking every single row.

I called the sheriff at Q's. Q's is a bar, billiards, and bowling establishment. Very loud. We didn't want to arouse curiosity by having the dispatcher come on over his walkie-talkie, so that's why I just called him directly. The sheriff got on the phone.

"Sheriff," I said.

"Hello? Can't hear you, you'll have to speak up, ma'am."

"Sheriff, it's me, Torie," I said. I raised my voice a bit, but not a lot. It's not like the person in the cornfield could hear me.

"Torie, do we have a show?" he asked.

"We got a show," I answered him. "Now. Get over here now."

"On my way."

As I hung up the phone, I looked out into the field. There was nobody there. Surely they couldn't have left. Maybe they realized what was up and decided to leave while they could.

I raced down the steps, which was hard to do considering it is a very narrow spiral staircase. I stopped with my hand on the back door to my aunt's two-hundred-year-old farmhouse. What was I doing? I couldn't run out into the cornfield and say, "Don't leave until the sheriff gets here." I'd probably end up dead. It would only take the sheriff five minutes to get here, especially if he floored it. But I could be dead in that time, too.

I went to the basement door. "Psst, Deputy Miller. There's somebody out in the cornfield." No answer.

So what could I do to keep him on the property?

There was nothing I could do. I strained to look out the window in the kitchen. Nothing. I couldn't see anybody anywhere.

I opened the back door and stepped out on the porch. I caught a glimpse of somebody down on all fours. I was fairly certain that it was Lanny Lockheart, especially after what Eleanore had told me earlier. If Yvonne was the killer, nobody would have shown up because she was in jail. Whoever it was, he was definitely looking for something. He was convinced that something was in the cornfield. Knowing Aunt Emily, there were probably all sorts of things. She had the strangest ideas of what made good fertilizer.

I stood around on the porch, trying to hide behind the swing and the porch furniture, for at least two minutes. All the sounds on the farm became very loud. The cows seemed to moo more than usual. The chickens clucked louder. The geese were squealing. Did they always make this much noise or were they aware that something was up?

I went back to the basement steps. "Hey, Ralph? You down there?"

Sheriff Brooke and Deputy Duran walked up behind me from the back porch and I stifled a scream. It came out as a squeal instead. I rolled my eyes at Sheriff Brooke. That was my way of saying thanks for scaring the pee out of me. They must have parked down the road and ran up to the house because I didn't hear their squad car. I hadn't heard them walk up the porch steps or open the screen door to the kitchen, either.

They headed into the cornfield, their guns drawn. Sheriff Brooke walked slowly with his gun pointed at the ground, Duran's was pointed in the direction of the sky. Great, they'd end up shooting each other. I just knew they would.

About a minute went by without a sound. Then I heard some scrambling, figures darting back and forth. I think I counted three uniforms. That made me feel better. Three against one. Deputy Miller must have seen the person out in the field when I was on the phone and went outside before I ever got down the steps. Then a shot fired.

I had not thought that maybe the bad guy had come with a gun.

Moans came from the cornfield, and I panicked. I ran in the house and got my uncle's twelve-gauge shotgun off of his rack. Ammunition. Where did Uncle Ben keep his ammunition?

More sounds came from outside while I was running around the house trying to find the ammunition. Think. Think. Where did he get the ammo when he went to shoot the coyote? He walked in the door, went to the rack, and walked into the hallway and . . .

The basement. I opened the door and on a shelf immediately to my left were boxes of shells of various sizes for various guns. I found the right ones, loaded the twelve-gauge, and went out to the back porch.

"Sheriff?" I yelled. "I'm armed! Don't worry about me!"

It occurred to me that he'd be more concerned now than he was before. The shotgun was bigger than I was. But I could shoot it. I had on many occasions. I'd been skeet shooting with my uncle, not to mention the umpteen times I'd shot soda cans off of stumps with my cousins. I could probably even hit something.

My hands were shaking, but not nearly as much as my knees, and I never wanted to be someplace else more than I wanted to be right now. Well, there was one other time, but that's another story.

Suddenly a figured emerged from the corn. It was Lanny Lockheart. He looked at me funny at first. And then he realized that this wasn't a random police check that caught a prowler, but that he'd been set up. He had a small pistol in his hand, and my heart beat wildly. Was Sheriff Brooke dead? Oh, God.

Lanny's eyes looked straight into mine.

The shotgun was raised at my hips. With a twelve-gauge I could kill him, without raising it to my face and taking careful aim. As long as I hit something.

But I didn't want to kill him. I couldn't kill him. I'd never killed anything deliberately with malice. Except spiders.

His gun was at his side. I could shoot him before he got it raised.

"Put the gun down," I said. "This is a really stupid thing to die for."

"You have no idea what consequences your actions will have," he said to me.

"There is no treasure, Mr. Lockheart. There are no consequences that I will have to deal with. You people need to get out of fantasyland." I saw Deputy Duran walking up slowly behind Lanny. And the short, stocky build of Deputy Miller came from the side. "You didn't really have an alibi, did you? You gave Andrew's name thinking he'd back you up, which he did, although not very convincingly. You dug up the grave. You'd be big enough to carry Camille through her house and force her into the garage. But who ran me off the road? Let me guess. Andrew? How about Yvonne?"

Fear played across his face. "You leave her out of this," he said. "You can't prove that she did anything. She was in Chicago the night Marie died. She didn't do it."

"But she did run me off the road, didn't she?"

"Yvonne is my wife," he said.

"Which would explain how the documents got in her car," I said. "You must have been frantic when you learned that she was arrested for the attempted murder of Camille."

"I'm not saying anything else," he said and started to raise his gun.

"I wouldn't, Mr. Lockheart," Duran said from behind him. Lanny dropped his gun to the ground, but his eyes never left me the whole time.

I set the shotgun on the floor of the porch and took off running toward the cornfield. I had to get to the sheriff.

"Sheriff?" I ran past the dry cornstalks trying to see into the rows, but it was nearly dark now. "Sheriff! Answer me, you big jerk!"

"Over here," I heard him say faintly.

All I could think of was a gut wound. And I wasn't so sure I was prepared for that kind of blood. I'm not very strong stomached when it comes to that sort of thing anyway. All I have to do is look at a freshly stitched wound and I get light-headed.

The blood ran from my face when I saw him lying on the ground with his belt pulled tight across his thigh. He'd been shot in the leg, and there was blood darkening the material of his pants. Sweat beaded on his forehead and he looked incredibly pale. I didn't think that it was due to lack of blood, but more from pain and fear.

"My God," I said. I knelt down next to him. I was so relieved that he wasn't dead.

"Oh, no," he said.

"What?"

"You almost hugged me," he said.

"I did not."

"Yes you did. I could see it."

"Did not."

"You wanted to hug me, you were so glad to see me alive."

"Believe me, it's only for my mother's sake."

"You really hate me that bad?" he asked.

"I don't hate you," I said. "I'm just not sure how fond of you I am."

He smiled at me and ruffled my hair. Why does everybody do that?

"I never gave it much thought," I said. "I was just relieved that I wasn't going to be looking at a dead body."

"Well, if you don't shut up and get me out of here, I may get dead."

NEW KASSEL GAZETTE

THE NEWS YOU MIGHT MISS
by Eleanore Murdoch

This year's apple dumpling recipe winner is . . . ME! I won! Can you believe it? Thank you everybody who voted for me. It was my grandmother's recipe and I am only too proud to pass it on to you wonderful people.

On a more somber note. I have always thought that our beloved New Kassel was a safe haven, a world away from the real one. In recent months some things have happened to make me change the way I looked at New Kassel. Has the real world finally got so large and intrusive that it has finally come to rest its ugly head in my wonderful town? The answer is no. There have always been ugly things and "real world" problems going on, just on a smaller scale. I was blind to them. Now I see them. I don't mean to scare anybody, but please, lock your doors at night. We have so many strangers from all over the country come to visit us. You never know when one will mean us harm.

And on a much happier note, nobody has claimed Fritz. So, the O'Sheas have a dog! It's rumored that even the mayor likes this animal.

Until next time.

Eleanore

Thirty

I wore my 1860s hoopskirt. It was easily something that
Melanie Wilkes would have worn in *Gone With the Wind*. It
was a peach dotted swiss gown with bishop sleeves and a
diamond-shaped belt. I wore no hat only because the one that
went with this dress had a torn tassle and was being repaired.

Rachel and Mary had just talked Sylvia into having "olden
days dresses" made for them so that on special days like
this they could be festive. We hoped to have them ready by
Christmas.

I stood outside on the steps of the Gaheimer House, awaiting my next tour. My mother and the sheriff were in matching
wheelchairs. He could have used crutches, but he thought this
was much more romantic. He would change his mind when she
beat him at wheelchair drag races.

"Has anybody seen Rudy?" I asked.

"He was at the pie-eating contest last time I saw him," Sheriff Brooke said.

"He won, no doubt," I said.

"How do you know?"

I just smiled at him.

I was about to go inside when Andrew Wheaton came walking up to the steps of the Gaheimer House. He was casual today: jeans and a pink polo shirt.

"I just checked out of the Murdoch Inn," he said. "I can't tell you how disturbed I am about all of this."

"What do you think, Mr. Wheaton? Lanny denies killing Marie on purpose. He swears it was the result of a fight. Do you think he's capable of premeditated murder?"

"I don't know," he said. "I certainly wouldn't have thought of him as a grave robber, but he was."

"That was sort of my thought, as well. I suppose we'll never know."

"I was wondering," Andrew began and then hesitated.

"If I know the location of the treasure?"

"Yes," he said and shuffled his feet. Sheriff Brooke raised his eyebrows.

"Do you really believe that there is a treasure?" I asked.

"With my very being," he said.

"Well, I'll tell ya, Mr. Wheaton. Since you're such a believer. Yes. I know the location of the treasure."

"Torie!" Sheriff Brooke said.

"Relax, Sheriff. See, I don't believe there is a treasure. I think these societies prey on the fact that people want to believe in the outrageous. A conspiracy is the first thing that will get people all fired up. If the Merovee Knights spread it around that there was no treasure or that there was a treasure but it was found long ago or wasn't what anybody expected, they'd have no members. Tons of money is spent on this very type of thing and it's nothing but a hoax. But if there truly is a treasure, Mr. Wheaton isn't going to kill me to get it because then the location goes with me. Nobody else knows where it's at," I lied. "And I've not written it down."

Andrew smiled at me.

"It's a classic standoff, hey, Mr. Wheaton?" I asked.

"Were we close?" he asked.

"Not at all," I lied again.

Rudy and Eleanore crossed the street then, coming toward us. Rudy had cherry stains on his blue T-shirt. His stomach protruded beyond his belt, stretched in an obvious glutonous display.

"How many pies did you eat?" I asked.

"Don't ask," he moaned.

"Oh, Torie," Eleanore said. "He was positively disgusting."

"So, you won?"

Rudy nodded.

"Congratulations. This is four years in a row."

"What did you win?" Andrew asked.

"A dozen cherry pies," Rudy answered.

Andrew laughed and looked at me once more. "If you ever want to divulge that information, look me up."

"If I ever want to divulge that information, I will tell Camille and Sister Lucy," I said.

He nodded at me and left.

"What was he talking about?" Eleanore asked.

"Oh, nothing," I said and giggled. Mom was trying hard to keep a straight face.

"You're really not going to tell anybody?" the sheriff asked.

"Nope."

Just then Sylvia stuck her head out the door. "Victory! Get in here right now. You have tourists waiting!" She looked to Sheriff Brooke and snarled, "And, you, look at the display you're making of yourself. Pretending to be handicapped. You should be ashamed. And, Rudy, you look positively like a pig!"

I laughed heartily.

"And, Eleanore," she went on, "what are you staring at?

What are you doing here? If you're not going to work, then go and sit in your own house and loaf. Don't instill discord in the troops!"

Eleanore was flustered. "Well, I never!"

Things were back to normal in New Kassel, Missouri. I wasn't sure if that was good or bad.

MacPherson, Rett.
    A veiled antiquity :
a novel

10/98